Christopher Fowler lives and works in London, where he runs a movie promotion company. He is the bestselling author of ROOFWORLD, RUNE and RED BRIDE, and of another urban horror anthology, THE BUREAU OF LOST SOULS. He is the creator of the comic character Menz Insana, and is currently completing DARKEST DAY, and another anthology, SHARPER KNIVES. If he didn't go out so much, he'd write more.

Praise for Christopher Fowler

ROOFWORLD
'A major new chiller writer bursts onto the scene, half-way between J.G. Ballard and Stephen King.' *Newsday*
'Rich with startling imagery, a brooding and highly entertaining depiction of a seductive shadow city.' *Kirkus*

THE BUREAU OF LOST SOULS
'Manages to unnerve, disgust and amuse in equal measure.' *Time Out*
'Clever horror storie[...] uppance.' *Sunday Ti[...]*

RUNE
'A ripping read.' *The[...]*
'Wonderful characte[...] phere, and it all work[...]*
'Easily the best horror novel I've read in a very long time.' *Oxford Times*
'As a novel within the genre of horror and the supernatural, it's about the best I've ever had the pleasure to read.' *Houston Chronicle*

CITY JITTERS

CHRISTOPHER FOWLER

WARNER BOOKS

A *Warner* Book

First published in Great Britain in 1986
by Sphere Books Ltd
This revised edition published in 1992
by Warner Books

Copyright © Christopher Fowler, 1986, 1992

The right of Christopher Fowler to be identified as author of
this work has been asserted by him in accordance with the
Copyright, Designs and Patents Act 1988.

ISBN 0 7088 5377 3

Typeset by Leaper & Gard Ltd, Bristol
Printed and bound in Great Britain by
BPCC Hazells Ltd
Member of BPCC Ltd

Warner Books
A Division of
Little, Brown and Company (UK) Limited
165 Great Dover Street
London SE1 4YA

Contents

Contents

Darkness In Daylight

It's hard to scare people in sunshine.

Blue skies, bird-song and busy streets break the spell. Horror writers need an atmosphere of thunder, graveyards and bats, but these images have been cheapened with overuse. And, really, these days they're not too believable. Murderers don't wait for the height of the storm before attacking. (They do murder more in the heat, though. When the temperature touched 102 degrees in New York last July, there was a record number of bizarre, pointless killings.)

Horror is beset by cliché. Book jackets show rats, skulls, knives and snakes. In movies, there's always a two-foot-high mist in graveyards. (Excuse me but I live in the city — we don't *get* mist, okay?)

And so we must find new ways to frighten. One method is to invest a mundane image with new menace. Peter Benchley and Steven Spielberg made going to the seaside a traumatic experience for a whole generation with *Jaws*. The West London locations of many J.G. Ballard tales are now as unforgettable as the stories themselves. Ruth Rendell's characters are as familiar as the folk next door — but much more disturbing. George Sluizer's superb film *The Vanishing* shows that terror can lurk in a busy, sunlit service station.

1

Another way to frighten is by creating bizarre, shocking new images. In *The Brute*, Joseph Conrad's mass murderer is more evil than Hannibal Lecter, and bigger too — it's a ship. In Peter Greenaway's *The Cook, The Thief, His Wife And Her Lover*, a couple are locked naked inside a truck filled with flyblown rotting meat. Stephen King's *It* has an evil clown hiding inside a drain, for God's sake.

A good writer avoids clichés. A great writer invents new ones. Forget the bats and belfries — let's see some new fears.

All of which leads me to this book.

As the strands of our daily lives cross-hatch and blur together with increasing complexity, literary genres are merging to create their own hybrids. That's why I mix horror, fantasy and mystery in modern-day settings. My stories are urban, slightly paranoid, usually sprinkled with a little black humour.

London figures largely as the backdrop, and frequently acts as a catalyst for supernatural events. I plan to explore the past, present and future lives of this fascinating city, populating it with characters real enough to exist, yet sufficiently steeped in the fantastic to be able to reveal new shadows within its ancient buildings.

These tales were my first attempt at defining horror's new perimeters. Although I now write novels, I always return to the short story. It's the best place to experiment, and the best way to learn what scares us both. Short stories inspire terrible thoughts. Stick around — I'll see what I can come up with.

Christopher Fowler
London, 1991

2

Citylink One

From the sunbleached sierras they come, blasting across the frozen fjords, down through desolate salt-caked steppes to scream high above the streaming gulf; the wild winds of the world roar from every far corner of the planet, to meet in a mighty maelstrom halfway up Tottenham Court Road, just outside Lasky's Video discount shop.

The new precinct there had looked very stylish when it was just a balsawood model standing in the foyer of the town hall, thought Norris. Models, however, fail to reveal the airstreams which form around them when they are translated to full-scale bricks and mortar, and this particular model had failed spectacularly, for the hurricane-like winds which blared about the new columns and architraves of the precinct created a Bermuda Triangle into which even the most hardened shoppers were careful not to stray. Paul Norris, a senior partner of the design consultants Norris & Damp, had been tacking in a southerly direction when the edge of the tornado caught his portfolio and threw it against his face. A moment later he had become trapped in a spinning, howling funnel of

3

takeaway boxes, Coke cartons and chip wrappers. It was as if he had suddenly been pushed through to some alternative dimension; Where The Litter Goes. He emerged from the other side of the tempest with his hair standing on end and a crisp bag stuck to his jacket.

Trudging through the grey London streets, hopelessly attempting to hail a cab, he felt completely at odds with the city in which he had spent his entire adult life. It was as if the accumulated knowledge which had been passed down through the memories of the city's inhabitants over the centuries had recently come to a grinding halt. London still rushed and buzzed around him, but Norris could no longer feel the warmth and wisdom generated by all this energy. He could no longer find its heart. In its place was a new kind of darkness. It wasn't so much that people were fearful of mugging, rape or burglary, but that they were disinterested in such attacks on others. The city was grinding down, running out, trapping its inhabitants like ants beneath a rock.

He studied the surrounding peninsulars of concrete, the traffic-bashed bollards, the Red Routes, Double Yellows, Grids and Bus Lanes, and wondered how traffic had come to take priority over people, how efficiency had achieved a higher value than elegance. Tomorrow he would be visiting Florida on a fact-finding tour of the new Miami Design Centre, and hopefully he would return with some idea of how America had learned to incorporate advanced technological stress-factors within its cities. He was also hoping to get a tan. He had never visited the United States before, but beyond certain cultural differences he was expecting no real surprises. A city was a city wherever you went, right?

4

He threw one last despairing glance at Tottenham Court Road and descended into the crowded tube station.

Alighting from the train, Norris was swept along the platform and up the stairs with the rush-hour commuters to be expelled from the subway exit like a champagne cork leaving a bottle.

Slowing himself to an eventual halt on the bustling sidewalk, he smoothed down his straggling fair hair and looked up. Tall glass office buildings crushed in on every side. The evening sky provided a roof of slate. Around him secretaries and clerks, waitresses and busboys, executives and shop assistants passed in a slipstream, rushing to get home. Norris set down his travel bag and cleared the sheen of sweat from his brow. Then he dug into his jacket pocket, looking for the shred of paper on which the woman had written the hotel address. Behind him there was a thud as somebody stumbled over his bag.

'Goddamn tourists!' said the man to his colleague, glaring angrily at Norris as he dusted the knees of his trousers.

Is it that obvious I'm from out of town? thought Norris. Looking at his clothes, he supposed that it was. To begin with, he was the only person on the street wearing an overcoat and scarf, an unusual choice of clothing considering the temperature `was 102 degrees. When his connecting flight had been delayed by thunderstorms, Norris had been dumped at JFK airport for an overnight stay in New York. As his suitcases were being retained by the airline, he was left with just his travel bag, which contained a pair of deck shoes, a snorkel, three books and several audio cassettes to go with the Walkman he had forgotten to pack. Norris was not a highly experienced traveller.

'Watch out, buddy.' Two enormous black men in overalls pushed past Norris with a large wooden crate and vanished into a department store. Realising that he was in the way, Norris pulled his bag over against the wall and rummaged through it, finally producing a crushed scrap of paper. The ink had run slightly, making the lettering illegible. It looked like *Hotel Centaur*, but it couldn't be, could it? *Central*, perhaps. And was that Second Avenue or Third? No telephone number. Great, and it was just starting to get dark. Instead of arriving in Miami's giant bowling alley of an airport in time for cocktails, he was in the wrong city and the wrong part of town, thanks to a bus driver's refusal to split a fifty dollar bill or accept a traveller's cheque.

Norris looked at the piece of paper again. The word had to be *Central*. Watching his altercation with the bus driver earlier, the woman next to him had recommended a small, inexpensive hotel which she said was just a couple of stops away on the subway. She had even written down the address for him. Norris had been warned about New Yorkers, but she seemed normal enough. She wasn't drinking out of a bag, and her shoes matched. He had decided to trust her.

Norris pushed the piece of paper into his pocket and swung the travel bag onto his shoulder. 'Excuse me,' he called to a sharp-suited businesswoman who was passing by, 'I wonder if you could tell me ...'

The woman looked at him as if she had been accosted by a tramp and hurried on, unfaltering in her stride.

'Erm, excuse me ...' He attempted to hail a grey-suited banker type. 'Could you direct ...' The banker flicked a brief blank glance at Norris, but could have been looking through him at the wall for all the acknowledgment he gave. Norris frowned. It shouldn't be this hard to communicate. After all, he thought, we speak the same language. He decided to walk on. She had told him the hotel was near the subway exit, so this could be the right street. Of course, there were several exits to the subway …

As he walked, he studied the buildings. Pawnshop, dry cleaners, Chinese restaurant, porno cinema showing a double bill (*Dicked Tracy* and *Twin Cheeks*), record store, gun shop, car wash. There was no way that this could be a socially acceptable part of town. In the car wash, leather strips flipped aside to reveal a glittering black Cadillac within, like the contents of a Fabergé egg.

He stepped from the kerb and passed the entrance to a large concrete tunnel. What was this? He stopped and looked down into the darkness. As he stood peering in, the noise of a car engine grew until a vehicle suddenly burst from the entrance, nearly slamming Norris over the hood. He managed to throw himself to one side as the Mazda took off into the traffic with a squeal of hot rubber.

Crossing to the safety of the far sidewalk, Norris was drawn back to the entrance of the underground garage. There was something disturbing about these gloomy repositories that, for him at least, defied rationality …

Left Hand Drive

A messenger could have made the delivery just as easily. Packham, passing between the shadowed buildings of the business district, picked up the envelope and checked the address. As the heat of the day ebbed into evening, cool fingers of air ruffled his hair, and he set the envelope back on the seat beside him. Packham figured he'd save the cost of a messenger and detour past 5454 West Plaza on his way home, nosing his big blue Oldsmobile between the cars parked in front of the area's many cocktail bars and restaurants.

The building turned out to be typical of so many of the new office blocks being constructed across Los Angeles, vast and characterless, the symmetry of its endless white walls broken by giant squares of bleak mirrored glass. He slowed the car as it approached the silent fountains in the plaza forecourt. Although the working day had ended over an hour ago, there were no parking spaces to be had on the street. Behind crackling neon signs, hidden beyond darkened glass, executives sat, presumably, theorising on the office politics of the day. Perhaps he would stop for a beer before tackling the freeway tonight. As much as he resented having to pay two and a half bucks for a five-minute call, Packham sighed and turned the vehicle along the west face of the building until he reached the underground parking facilities. Snatching a card from the striped yellow ticket meter, he barely waited for the metal arm to raise in front of him before pushing down on the accelerator.

He was in luck. The enormous concrete cavern below him yielded a parking space in the first underground level. Packham edged the Oldsmobile in between a Toyota truck and a Volkswagen. He opened the car door gingerly to prevent scratching his new paintwork, and looked about. Throughout the car park giant metal signs were set into the concrete support posts, their colour-coded reflective messages aiming visitors at banks of elevators and escalators.

It always amazed Packham how these vast underground car parks managed to remain as antiseptically clean as the buildings above them. And indeed, the tower block overhead proved to be a model of its kind. The muted pastel carpeting in the foyer ended against tall, pale marble-faced walls. Lettered tables, gold on black, revealed the presence of hundreds of small companies. The obligatory modern sculpture, an arrangement of steel shards, towered over low purple seating arranged in the reception area. Packham patted the envelope in his jacket. It felt powerful and hard, as only a lawsuit could when slipped into smooth manila. Kimberly Inc. had repeatedly failed to pay on time, and now they would suffer the consequences of their bad business policy. Fair was fair. The same set of rules applied to everyone. Aside from that, it was the easiest way to make money that Packham was aware of.

After depositing the envelope with the night receptionist, his heels ticking on the glistening marble runway across the foyer, Packham returned to the elevator bank and touched the pressure-sensitive 'DOWN' button. Colleagues thought that he spent too much money on lawyers, that he knew. The elevator arrived. He stepped in. Lawyers were worth spending money on. How else would he discover the little legal loopholes through which money poured into his business? Not a vast amount, to be sure, but certainly enough to keep Packham's otherwise ailing company afloat. When the elevator arrived at 'P1', the doors slid open and Packham found himself facing his Oldsmobile. He congratulated himself on an energy-saving piece of parking. Seating behind the wheel once more, Packham decided to stop off on the way home for a cocktail or three, secure in the knowledge that his wife would be content if he even appeared at all that evening. Turning around in his seat with one hand on the wheel, Packham looked out through the back window in an attempt to locate the car park's exit teller. He assumed that, as in most places of this kind, the exit would be at the far end of a one-way system designed to keep traffic flowing in a circle around the garage. Outside he could see the sidewalk darkening to soft crimson as night began to fall.

Packham backed the car out into the lane ahead and followed the arrows painted on the floor as they led around to his left. Slowly guiding the big old car between columns of parked vehicles, he turned on the radio to catch the early evening traffic news.

'And there's a two-mile tailback on the southbound lane of the Hollywood freeway tonight at Gower junction, so try and avoid that route if you can. Now it's time for the latest weather ...'

Ahead, the floor arrows continued to point around to the left. Packham coasted the Olds in an arc, searching for the familiar yellow stripes of the exit booth. The arrows led down a narrow ramped tunnel to the floor below. That couldn't be right. Packham leaned forward and looked up through the windscreen at the top of the tunnel. The sign was large, clear and straightforward. It read simply 'EXIT' — and there was a reflective arrow below it pointing straight on. Irritated, he eased the car down the tunnel to the floor below. Here there were two signs, one repeating the message 'EXIT', and the other which read 'MONTHLY PARKING ONLY'. Packham curved the car in the direction of the exit arrows.

On this level there were fewer cars, and the ones which were here looked as if they had been for quite a while. Overhead, the lighting had grown dimmer, the neon strips having been replaced with dusty, flickering panels recessed into the ceiling. Packham slowed the car down for a moment and rested his arms on the wheel. It seemed that he had made a complete circuit around the second floor of the car park, but still no exit teller was visible. Anyway, how could there even be one on the second floor down? Weren't they always near the entrance? The building was of fairly new design. Perhaps this was a new system. Ahead, the arrowed lane continued for five hundred yards and then split into two directions. Above the split a sign hung from the ceiling, difficult to read at this distance. Packham gunned the accelerator in annoyance and pulled up at the painted forking of the ways. The sign read 'LONG TERM PARKING' and had an arrow beneath it pointing right. Below this it said, once again, 'EXIT', and this was joined with a similar arrow pointing left. Finally, thought Packham as he swung the car to the left — only to reach the corner and discover to his amazement that the arrows were pointing downwards once more to a ramp leading to the floors below.

Packham was not an irrational man. He was sure that the architectural quirks of this particular building were merely an annoying development of the crazy new fire regulations. Even so, he felt a brief quiver in the pit of his stomach when the radio began crackling with static as he descended the ramp. Down here there were only a handful of cars filling the parking stalls in dusty clutches. Some looked as if they had been here for a very long time indeed. Old newspapers were plastered against the windshields and tyres, and dust had left thick lines of grey along chrome trims and wipers. Cruising slowly along the arrowed lane, Packham leaned forward, searching the concrete columns for any further instructions for locating the exit ramps.

Some of the cars he was now passing looked as if they had not been disturbed for months. The Olds crawled past a rusting Chevy Vega, then a weather-beaten '59 Chevrolet, its vast tailfins caked with streaks of dirt. On the radio the static now over-powered the station announcer's voice. Packham clicked it off with annoyance. Obviously he had missed a turn somewhere. He must be near the basement of the car park down here.

Flickering panels of light slid over the windshield of the Oldsmobile as it passed each crusted metal hulk. In the distance glowed a two-way sign, too far away as yet to be deciphered in the gloom.

Packham pulled the car up beneath it and idled the engine. A leaking water pipe overhead had streaked the notice with rust. One side read: 'CARPORT CLOSES AT 9.00PM'. The other side read: 'EXIT'. As on all the other floors, there were two lanes ahead, branching and curving off to the left and the right. Packham pulled his tie loose and unbuttoned his collar. He could feel the sweat dripping between his shoulderblades. The air was warm and heavy, and felt long undisturbed. Having had no luck following the exit signs, Packham decided to head in the opposite direction of the painted exit arrows, swinging the wheel of the Olds around to the left and accelerating once more. With growing horror he found the car descending its ramp again to the floor below.

Flicking on the main beam of his headlights, Packham hunched forward against the wheel, his forehead leaving condensation marks against the glass. The signs were fewer now, the lighting poor and sporadic. Several of the overhead light panels were missing, revealing tangles of dusty plastic wiring. Slowly the Oldsmobile wound downwards into the dark, past a rusted Ford Pinto with four flat tyres.

Ahead, he turned the wheel to avoid an abandoned Pontiac convertible, left at an angle across the centre of the lane, its slashed seats exposing contusions of ragged foam rubber. At the next corner, a sign had fallen down and lay amidst old rags and dust, its single word 'EXIT' pointing straight down into the earth.

The oppressive heat forced beads of sweat into Packham's eyes. He pulled the car over, shifted it into PARK and applied the handbrake. As he extracted his keys from the ignition, the sudden silence was so disturbing that he quickly reapplied his key and turned over the engine of the Olds once more. He looked at his watch. How long had he been down here? The luminous dial glowed faintly in the warm gloom. It appeared to read 7.50 — but that would mean he had been circling the garage for three quarters of an hour, and Packham knew that it couldn't have been more than ten minutes at the most. He ran his hand through his thinning brown hair, feeling the moisture that had gathered at the roots. It was stupid to continue following the signs. There was no way that the exit could be this far down. He had to go back the way he had come. Keeping in as tight a turning circle as possible, Packham drove across the empty parking spaces and headed back up the lane. He reached the foot of the ramp upwards to the next floor, and gently applied the accelerator. Slowly the car rose back up the ramp until it reached the abandoned convertible it had passed minutes before. Packham accelerated once more as the Olds passed under the flickering signs which had urged him downwards.

He passed the Pinto, passed another 'EXIT' sign pointing back the way he had gone, and overhead the lighting grew stronger and less patchy. Hopefully he tried the radio, but the deafening static forced him to turn it back off. In another moment he reached the base of the next ramp upwards. It seemed steeper than he remembered, and narrower. Surely it had to be the same one? Packham set his teeth and revved the engine. Ahead, at the top of the tunnel he could see the cool brilliance of the neon ceiling panelling. Halfway up the ramp, the engine died and the car began to roll slowly backwards.

Packham stared at the instrument panel in disbelief. He had plenty of gasoline. The battery was fully charged. Everything else read normal. Twisting in his seat, Packham guided the car back down the ramp and swung it in an arc at the bottom so that the vehicle faced forward once more. He turned off the ignition, waited a moment and tried the engine again. On the fourth try, the car drummed into life once more. Relief flooded through him. He had been meaning to take the car in for a service for two months now — he just hated shelling out to those bastards in the body shop

14

for wiping the engine with a damp rag and charging him a hundred and eighty dollars.

Edging the Oldsmobile around, Packham stepped on the gas and headed up the ramp again. As he reached the midway point of the tunnel, the engine coughed and failed. Only his previous experience kept Packham from running the trunk of the car into the concrete wall behind. Once more he parked at the bottom of the ramp and clicked off the ignition. This time the engine failed to turn over until the battery was nearly dead.

The choice facing him was a simple one. Either he had to leave the car here and walk up — which as far as he was concerned was out of the question — or go back down and continue to follow the signs to the exit. Packham reached into the back seat and pulled a Kleenex from the door pocket. Mopping his forehead, he coasted the Olds gently around and along the arrowed lane, back past the Pinto and down the narrow concrete ramp into the gloom of the floor below. As he passed his previous turning point, it occurred to Packham that he had been traversing the lanes of this underground crazyhouse for quite a while now, and as the car passed beneath a buzzing and spluttering light panel he peered once more at his watch. The face now read: 8.35. That was impossible! He had looked at his watch in the foyer of the building above him at precisely 7.05, and again — just a few minutes ago, surely? He *couldn't* have been down here for an hour and a half!

The Oldsmobile passed a cluster of vehicles which looked as if they had not been moved for five years. An old Plymouth with a smashed front windshield, a small brown Fiat with its passenger door torn off, a burned out Chevy Nova, a Toyota Selica with no hood or headlights. Veering away from the arrowed lane before him, Packham angled the car across the lot towards its farthest side. He must have been travelling faster than he realised, for the tyres screamed in the tomblike emptyness of the block.

Set in the far wall was a dark square hole, and above, yet another 'EXIT' sign. By the light reflecting against the angled ceiling, Packham could tell that the ramp beyond the sign led downwards once more. There had to be an end to the number of floors available for parking, even for an office building as large as the one overhead. Taking care to keep the car engine revving gently, he entered the ramp tunnel. This one was definitely smaller than any of the others. The walls seemed to be pressing in against the sides of the car. They were mere inches further apart than the Olds. If he had wanted to open the doors of the car, he would not have been able to. As the floor levelled out once more, his headlights picked up the wreckage of destroyed and abandoned cars in the near pitch darkness. Above him flickered one single panelled light, its plastic cover shattered and dripping rusty water.

With a sudden shock, Packham realised that he was frightened. He was aware of a physical change in himself. His hands were oozing sweat, making the steering wheel slippery to hold. He wiped them on his slacks. His face was wet and cold, his heart beating way too fast. He could feel it pulsing through the dampness of his shirt. Looking at the speedometer he realised he was crossing the darkened floor at nearly forty miles an hour. The wheel slid in his hands. He shifted his gaze to the windshield just in time to see the light from his main beam reflected on the pale blue roof of an upturned Chrysler before the Oldsmobile slammed into it.

It seemed to Packham that some time was lost before he remembered touching his bruised forehead and climbing out of the car to shakily survey the damage. His right fender was crumpled beyond repair. Its headlight had gone out, leaving the single offside lamp to throw its amber light across the floor. Something under the hood was hissing. Metal ticked to a stop. Without daring to see how much damage he had done, Packham banged the hood flat and jumped back into the driver's seat. Squealing the car into reverse and then punching it forward around the wreck, he could feel the twisted front fender dragging and tearing at his nearside tyre. Ahead, the single beam of the Oldsmobile illuminated a barely legible sign: 'EXIT LEFT', with its inevitable entrance to a downward ramp. As the car scraped into the passageway, the hissing under the hood grew louder until something split with a bang and the engine ceased to turn.

With mounting horror, Packham realised that the scraping noise around him was caused by the walls of the ramp, which were now touching both sides of the car as it coasted downward under the pull of its own weight. He hammered at the wheel now, praying that the car would not hit an obstacle and stop. The car was surrounded by crushing hot blackness as its single beam picked out the way ahead. The ramp was longer than any previous, and steeper. By the angle of the car, Packham could tell that the incline of the ramp was growing instead of lessening.

Now there was a new scraping sound, from above. The roof was low here, so low that in places it touched the top of the car. As the scraping increased in volume, Packham knew that the tunnel was so narrow now that any second the car would slow down and stop, unable to move any further.

The next instant he felt his stomach turn sourly over as the scraping ended and the car ground to a complete standstill. Tearing at the handle, Packham flung his full weight at the door, with no effect. Sheer panic overwhelmed him as he slammed his elbow at the side window, finally shattering it and sending spears of glass into the tendons of his arm. Beyond the window, less than two or three inches away, was the streaked grey concrete of the all-enclosing ramp wall. Suddenly aware of the searing pain in his right arm, Packham slumped over the wheel and cried.

Time passed until Packham was snapped back into panicky attention by the flickering of his remaining headlamp. He raised his head from the steering wheel and stared out of the windshield. Ahead, pressed against the crumpled hood of the car was the sheer concrete wall of a dead end. The headlamp flickered off, then on again. Packham craned his head up at the far edge of the light pool, where something glittered. It was the reflective lettering of yet another 'EXIT' sign. As the light began to fade from the headlamp and blackness shrank the circle of dimming brightness, Packham strained to read the words sprayed below the sign in crimson paint, a final message. It said simply:

'ON THE LEFT HAND OF GOD SITS SATAN'.

With a ping, the headlamp and instrument panel lights went out.

In the silence and the darkness, Packham heard a new noise.

Citylink Two

'Hey, Mister! You lost?' The cab driver, overweight, unshaven and wearing a Hawaiian shirt open to the waist, was leaning from the window of his car calling to Norris. Salsa music played on the radio behind him.

'I'm looking for a hotel,' Norris called back. 'I have the address here on a piece of paper.' He brought the note over.

'Here, gimme dat.' The cabbie screwed up his eyes and stared hard at the paper, as if trying to decipher its message by psychic means.

'Oh, yeah,' he said unconvincingly. 'Yeah, I know where this place is. Get in, get in.' He reached out and opened the back door. Despite the presence of a meter, the vehicle didn't look much like a regular cab. Norris imagined customers didn't get much peace of mind being driven about in a badly rear-ended Pinto. The back seat dipped in the middle, the overstuffed ashtrays were releasing clouds of ash, and the driver was sitting behind a chicken-wire barrier. Norris sat back in his seat unhappily.

'How far away is this place?' he asked.

'Coupla blocks, but they're long blocks an' what with you carryin' that there bag ...' He slammed the car noisily into gear and pulled away from the kerb with a jerk. 'Your first time in town?' he called, removing his eyes completely from the road and looking over his shoulder.

'Yes,' answered Norris. 'Is it that obvious?'

'Are you kiddin'?' The driver snorted with laughter, then wiped his nose with his hand. 'You're dressed like Sherlock Holmes. You know, the limey fag detective.'

'Pardon me?' Norris hung onto the armrest as the cab tilted alarmingly around a corner.

'Talkin' a fashion, you like the seat covers?'

'They're, er —' Norris's voice trailed off as he stared in disbelief at the pink leopard-skin seats.

'I recovered 'em myself. Had a guy in the back slit his fuckin' wrists, ruined the interior. Had nine bucks in his wallet. I still can't get it outta the carpet. Seats needed recoverin' anyways, the number of people who's had sex where you're sittin'.' Norris looked down between his feet at the darkly matted floor. Just then he remembered that he had no change smaller than a fifty-dollar bill. He tapped gingerly on the chicken wire.

'I'm sorry, but can you change a fifty?'

'Lessee here.' The driver rummaged inside his shirt and produced a couple of filthy, crumpled bills. 'I got twenty-five.'

'You mean this trip's going to cost me twenty-five dollars?'

'It's your choice, Mister, you're the one with the fifty. I can drive ya 'round the block until you've had your money's worth.'

Through the smeared window Norris could see tough-looking kids in gang jackets hanging out by a discount record store. An uncapped fire hydrant was pumping water into the gutter.

'Er, I don't think so.' Norris slumped back in the seat with a sigh. He lifted a corner of the seat cover, peered under it and hastily slapped it back down.

'Good, cuz we're here.' The driver slewed the cab over to the gutter and stopped so suddenly that Norris was thrown onto his knees. He pushed his fifty through the grille and received a twenty and a five in change.

'Hey, you enjoy your stay now.'

He barely had time to close the back door before the cab roared into life once more and took off into the traffic. Setting down his travel bag Norris looked up, expecting to see the front of the hotel.

Instead he found himself before a purple-painted massage parlour with rotating red lights attached to the windows.

He knew there was a reason why he never fully trusted cab drivers ...

Any Minute Now

The fat red candle guttered and went out. Damon clicked on one of the table lamps. He tipped his watch to the light and yawned. Beside him, Angela stretched.

'It's probably after midnight.'

'After midnight? Try one thirty.'

'God, I'm up in five hours. I must go.' Angela pulled her sweater back into shape and began looking around for her shoes. Damon retrieved one from beneath the couch and slipped it onto her foot.

'What time do you finish tonight?' he asked. Angela looked up, surprised.

'I come off duty at about seven ...' she began.

'How about letting me come and meet you? We can go for something to eat.'

'That would be ... nice.' Two nights in a row, thought Angela as she looked for her other shoe. 'I'm glad you liked the book.'

'I can't wait to read it. It's perfect.' Damon touched the cover of the volume on the cushion beside him. Angela was standing now, adjusting her skirt in the mirror.

'I'm sorry it wasn't something a little more exciting, but on a nurse's pay ...' She let the sentence fall and brushed her blonde hair out over her collar with a flick of her hand. Damon stood and circled his arms around her narrow waist.

'I've got all the excitement I need,' he smiled. 'Sounds like your cab.' A car had slushed to a stop beyond the front window.

Angela stopped by the hall stand on the way out to collect her hat. She adjusted the floppy brim above her eyes. Damon opened the front door. Goodbyes were exchanged while the cab, a nondescript blue Ford of ancient appearance, waited with its engine idling in the centre of the road. The driver was a black shadow beyond the rain-spattered windscreen.

'You'd better run or you'll get soaked,' said Damon, catching her shoulders and kissing her quickly. She moved her arms to his waist and rested her head on his chest, feeling its warmth through the wool of his sweater.

'Better not keep him waiting,' he said, adding softly. 'Love you.'

'Love you too,' Angela heard herself saying with some surprise. Embarrassed, she made a show of turning up her coat collar and tucking in the ends of her scarf.

'Well …' she said, turning at the doorway. 'Tomorrow, then.'

'Tonight, you mean,' he laughed.

And she was gone, out into the rain, across the pavement, now pulling at the back door of the minicab. The car pulled away, its door barely shut, and in another moment was lost to sight beyond the curve of the road.

Damon closed the front door and returned to the living room. Ashes glowed dully in the grate. The room smelled of warm, sweet wood, with just a trace of perfume. He refilled his glass with scotch, sank back down into the couch and picked up the book she had given him, a volume of Old English ballads. As he leafed through it, her image filled his mind, her lips curling at his terrible jokes, her eyes softening as she spoke. He had never met a woman more comfortable to be with. He rested his head on the back of the cushion and let his eyes close.

He did not turn around as she addressed him, but concentrated instead on the wet roads ahead. Angela gripped the back of the empty seat in front of her and cleared her throat.

'I want to go to Highbury, please. Avenall Road.'

'You'll have to show me the way when we get nearer.' The driver turned and looked at her blankly. His thick brown hair was greased flat across his forehead. He wore heavy tortoiseshell spectacles joined at the bridge of the nose with stickytape. He held her gaze for an endless moment, assessing her, then turned back to the wheel.

It was cold in the car. Angela could see her breath. She tucked her hands into her sleeves and sat back.

'Rotten night,' said the driver flatly. 'Wouldn't like to be outside right now.'

'No,' said Angela. 'Horrible,' she added.

She settled into the corner and looked out of the window. There were no people on the streets and very little traffic. Closed shop fronts. Boarded doorways. Nothing to see. She looked ahead, beyond the driver's wide shoulders. A cheap plastic hula girl hung from the rear view mirror by a necklace, knotted around its neck. There were a couple of creased photographs propped on the dashboard. Women, their features indistinct, one old, one young. Mother and wife?

'They've had to shut the southbound carriageway of the M1, you know,' the voice resumed.

Angela had a sudden feeling that he would talk through the entire journey now, intruding on private thoughts of the man she had held in the doorway.

'Have they?' Civility compelled her to reply. She watched the rivulets of water breaking and racing along the glass beside her, and felt the wheels beneath bite into the road as the car slowed before a red traffic light. The area through which they were passing had a dead, sealed-up feeling to it.

'It's the drains,' said the driver suddenly. His words were flattened by an accent she found hard to place. 'They can't take all this rain. The sewers fill up and flood the roads. It comes out some of the gratings around here like fountains.' The lights turned to green. He locked his fist over the gear stick, and the cab moved forward once more.

'There's a storm drain down the Mile End Road which takes your breath away sometimes.' He paused and considered. 'I blame the government for letting people put what they like down the toilets.'

Angela found it hard not to smile, wondering to herself what other odd views he held about everyday subjects. Sodium lamplight bathed the interior of the cab.

'Some would say,' he continued the moment Angela had decided he had finished, 'some would say that it's a basic human right. The right to put what you like down your toilet in the privacy of your own home. And I can't argue with that. But what I say is,' he paused to check the road before moving the car out of a junction, 'it should be biodegradable. Otherwise it will block everything up and cause no end of trouble.

Like them alligators.' He seemed satisfied with his own argument and fell silent.

They were passing through the business section of the city. Tall grey walls filled with sightless windows lined the street on either side. The streetlamps gave everything a sickly saffron sheen.

'Not that a nice young lady like you wants to talk about things down toilets.' The driver turned in his seat and stared at her. He was younger than she'd realised, his jaundiced face revealing few lines. He grinned suddenly, revealing dark crooked teeth.

'Nice area where I picked you up from,' he said. 'Lot of money there. That street, very pretty. Very posh.'

Beyond the window, the rain fell vertically, thrashing the car roof and chanelling along its gutters. There was nothing Angela could say in reply, even if she'd wanted to. She sank back into the seat and stared out at the night. Every time the vehicle accelerated, she felt the seat in front press into her knees, forcing them uncomfortably apart. She wished she'd sat behind the empty seat, but it was too late to move now.

'You at university?' asked the driver suddenly, as she was washing all thought from her mind. She tried to keep the irritation from her voice as she replied, but feared that it came through all the same.

'No. No, I'm not.'

''Cause I always wanted to go. But my mother was ill. There was nobody else to look after her, so I had to.' His voice hardened as he accelerated once more. 'I had to, for four years. That's her.' He tapped one of the creased photographs in front of him. 'Then, when it was too late for me to go, the cow died. Just like she'd been waiting.'

Angela wasn't sure whether or not a reply was expected. She decided to say nothing.

'Yes,' he sighed through his teeth as he tapped bitten nails on the steering wheel, 'some people find ways of getting at you right until they die.'

Angela let the driver's voice fade from her mind. She thought of Damon, of meeting him at the clinic where he lectured once a week, and how quickly she had realised that here, perhaps for the first time, was someone who really cared about her. Someone who continued to think of her afterwards, in the hours apart —

'*Fucking Bastards*!' The shock of the shout made her flinch and look up. A group of skinheads were hammering on the hood of the car as they passed in front of it, sauntering casually by, gesturing and calling insults.

'Sorry about that, but they get my goat, they really do. Acting like they own the world when they know nothing. Nothing at all.' He moved the car quickly forward, almost catching one of them in the leg. Angela sank down into her seat, not wishing to see who was outside, or what they might be doing. She disappeared into her coat, letting the rhythmic beat of the windscreen wipers lull her drowsily into private thoughts once more. They crossed over the Thames, the only vehicle on a rainswept bridge.

'Mind if I smoke?' She felt a hand tapping her on the knee. 'I said mind if I smoke?'

'Well, no … if you must,' Angela replied before she had even had a chance to consider the question. She wished she could learn to say what she really felt without feeling difficult, but it was too late now. He had already lit a cigarette, and the air in the cab was becoming dry and irritating. She opened the window a little and felt the rush of cold bringing icy spots of water with it.

'Yeah, like I said, I'd have gone to university, and then I'd have been able to get a good job, 'stead of pissing my life away night after night.'

The shock of the cold air brought Angela to full alertness. She listened to the driver and felt sorry for him in a vague, remote way. Outside, the street lamps were few and far between. They seemed to be passing amongst warehouses, brown and squat. Containers stood before shuttered garages. She suspected that they were somewhere at the back of King's Cross Station, but could not be sure. The car passed beneath a dripping railway arch.

'My sister had an easy time of it. First sign of my mother getting sick and she was off. Gone. Still, there you are.' As they emerged from the arch a fresh burst of rain drummed down on the roof. 'This bloody weather's getting worse.'

'How soon will we be there?' she asked, leaning forward so that he could hear her above the downpour.

'Don't worry, love, we're almost at Highbury Corner.' He turned around to face her and smiled. 'This way cuts about a quid off the bill. You'll soon be back in the warm.'

His smile seemed overquick and false as he caught her eyes with his. A moment later he was back at the wheel, wiping the windscreen with the sleeve of his jacket.

What a depressing job, thought Angela. But what else could the poor man do? His manner was halting and awkward. He obviously felt uneasy in the simplest of social situations. She found herself wondering if he had any friends, or whether he simply spent all his off-duty hours at home, watching old movies on a portable TV, making mugs of instant soup as she had done, sitting alone in the flickering greyness waiting for daylight ...

'Was that your boyfriend's house?'

'Well, yes ... it was.'

'Must have money. Must be nice for you,' he said, his voice tinged with bitterness. 'Probably handsome, too. Handsome people always have money, have you ever noticed that?' He paused for breath as he heaved the wheel around. 'Ugly people never get on. They can be witty, and intelligent, but no one will want to be around them. That's how this society is, you see. Thanks to American television and their perfect bloody people with their suntans and their teeth.' His voice showed anger now. He honked at the car in front and swerved around it to the clear roadway ahead.

'American women are the worst, all legs and hair-dos. They give you the come-on, let you get just close enough to see that they don't know you. Like they were TV characters.' His speech was faster now, and more mumbled, as if he talked like this when there was no one else in the car.

He was driving faster, too, through streets that were growing less and less familiar.

'That's the trouble with this city, you see.' He removed a hand from the wheel to stab the air. 'Everyone's so bloody important. All running from one appointment to the next, in their big glass tower blocks. People like me don't exist in their world.'

'Where are we?' asked Angela nervously. 'I don't know this area.' For all she knew he could be driving her around in circles, just to have someone on whom he could unburden himself.

Her interruption silenced him, and slowed down the car. Warmth flowed back into his voice.

'I'm sorry, sounding off like that. We'll be there in about two minutes.'

Angela turned and looked back out of the window. The roadway behind had tramlines embedded in it. Huge bales of shredded paper, bound with metal ties, stood stacked in railway arches. In the distance she thought she could hear a horn, like that of a tugboat.

'Are we still near the river?' she asked angrily. If he was trying to bump up the fare, she would make trouble with the cab company. She twisted the end of her scarf nervously in her lap.

'No, of course we're not near the river.'

He was lying. She could sense it in his voice, just as she could tell when Damon was trying to play a trick on her. What could she do? Ask him to stop the car and let her out? She would probably be in more danger outside, alone in a darkened wasteland inhabited by who-knew-what. Besides it was pouring with rain. She longed to be home, sitting in the warm with a cup of coffee, listening to the rain as it fell from the eaves.

Her feet were numb with cold. She shuffled them, trying to get the feeling back into her toes. She was sure he was lying. Suppose he grew violent? The cab companies hired some strange people as night drivers, but not maniacs, surely. She cursed her timidity, her inability to say something, to tell people that, yes, she *did* object to their smoking, their thinking they could make a fool of her and then charge her a fortune for the pleasure of it. Her thoughts were checked by a burst of laughter from the driver.

'Here,' he called back to her. 'You're probably thinking I'm trying to do you.' He turned the car into a side street in which most of the buildings were derelict and half demolished. 'Well, that's all right. You wouldn't be the first. Not by a long chalk.' He

30

chuckled to himself and shook his head. Angela pushed herself forward.

'Where are we?' she demanded. 'This doesn't look right at all.'

The car skidded slightly on the slickened tarmac as she stared through the glass. On one side a metal fence separated wasteland from the pavement. On the other stood the darkened doorways of a Victorian factory, movement heaving from within as derelicts turned in troubled sleep.

'Pull over at the first phonebox you see,' she called, rooting through her handbag in a fictitious search which covered her growing feeling of panic.

The car moved forward in silence. They coasted slowly through the rainblasted corridor of brick, past abandoned vehicles and over the cracked plastic of shattered bollards. At the end of the road, they came to a roundabout, ill lit but mercifully less claustrophobic than the pressing brown walls which had surrounded them for the last few minutes. Beyond the roundabout stood two telephone kiosks, their windows blackened with felt-tip hieroglyphics.

'Stop here and wait.' The driver silently obeyed, pulling the car up to the boxes until two wheels mounted the kerb. Angela fumbled in her purse for the right coins.

'Have one on me,' smiled the driver, passing her a warm coin.

As she stepped from the car to the callbox, she saw instantly that it was missing one door, one receiver and three telephone directories. She walked around to the other box and entered. Outside, the rain began to drop heavily and noisily once more.

In this box, littered with fried chicken bones and reeking of urine, she saw with amazement that the telephone had actually been melted, as if some demented thug had taken a blowlamp to it.

'I could have told you they weren't working,' said the driver redundantly as he leaned across and threw open the back door of the car. Angela slid onto the seat with angry haste. The figure in the driving seat closed his road map and slipped it into a sidepocket.

'You don't know where we are at all, do you?'

'I got confused,' he said, clicking out the overhead light and easing off the handbrake. 'I know where I am now. Sorry about that, I won't charge you for the detour.'

'I should hope not,' said Angela uneasily. 'Really.'

As the car sped on she stared out at the starbursts of light through the glass, seeing nothing but the occasional distortion of a wall or lamp post. When it finally pulled up to a halt, she was taken by surprise. The driver had idled the engine, clicked on the passenger light and opened his door. Climbing out, he walked to the back of the vehicle. Angela picked up her purse and pushed down on the chromium handle beside her right leg. The driver grinned. She stood and looked around. They were standing on a dockside, with causeways sloping down into rain-flattened water. The river before them was black and oily, the smell of rust and grease and freshly sheared metal permeating the air in spite of the rain. At first Angela failed to comprehend the scene before her. He stood with his legs apart, leaning slightly backwards as he smiled and nodded toward the tall blocks of stacked planks which lay beyond the car. He was mumbling to himself in a high, strange voice, rapidly and monotonously as if reciting some forgotten pagan litany.

Even as she felt herself starting to run, she knew he would catch her, pulling her down with his weight, onto the oil streaked concrete. She knew she was screaming now, a continuous shrill pitch as he revealed the thin blade of the pocket knife and arced it down toward her. She braced herself as she anticipated the icy heat of the metal sliding into her flesh, withdrawing and entering as smoothly as a lover. Here it came now ... slowly ...

But not a knife. It was the handle of the door, pressing against the bare skin of her arm. The sleeve of her sweater had ridden up where she had fallen to one side, driven to sleep by the drumming of the rain. Angela sat up smartly and wiped condensation from the window. Outside, she saw the brightly lit streets sloping gently upwards to Highbury. The driver glanced into his rear-view mirror.

'Don't worry, love. We're almost at Highbury Corner,' he said, his eyes flickering back to the road. In the cool of the rear compartment, Angela felt warmth flood through her body as she hugged herself tightly and released a long, slow breath.

The irritating trill of the telephone finally intruding into his sleep, Damon rolled over on the couch and lifted the receiver with the ends of his fingers. The book slipped from his lap to the floor with a thump.

'Mr Castle?' asked a male voice.

'Yes?' He cleared his throat and sat up. 'Speaking.'

'Just to say sorry for the delay on the cab you requested. The rain's slowing everything down tonight. He should be with you any minute now.'

Damon stared at the receiver. Beyond the window, a car horn sounded.

Citylink Three

'That ain't nowhere 'round here, man. That driver, he been playin' you for a fool, 'cause of your outfit.' The tall young man in the yellow and purple shellsuit handed the crumpled piece of paper back to Norris and smiled. A gold tooth glittered.

Norris was standing inside a video arcade trying to get directions. All around him, weird-looking kids hammered electronic machines or stood huddled in corners making suspicious deals. The place looked like a finishing school for delinquents. Empty Coca-Cola cups and popcorn cartons littered the floor. There was a hot, rancid smell in the air.

'How far am I from this place?' Norris shouted above the noise of the machine next to him, which had suddenly started to produce deafening electronic explosions. The tall young man shook his head vigorously.

'Like I said, I can't rightly say. But you jes' ask the doorman of the Lucky Seven Club. Ain't nowhere 'round here he don't know. You jes' tell him you a dumb tourist an' he'll give you directions.'

'Where is this club?' asked Norris, exasperated.

'You just around the corner, Jack. Go outta here,

left then straight ahead, you gon' come to it in about a hunnert yards.'

'Thanks for the information,' shouted Norris.

'Hey, no problemo. Have a good vacation. If you make it to the West Coast, don' forget to visit Universal Studios.' He waved as Norris retreated across the arcade floor. 'An' mind your skinny white ass in this neighbourhood,' he added with a laugh.

As he passed between the wailing, beeping machines, Norris felt sure that people were staring at him. He stuck out like a sore thumb, sweating inside dark winter clothes while everyone else wore shorts and trainers. He casually slid his hand into his pocket and checked his wallet as several mean-looking kids sputtered with laughter behind him.

Against the glass exit doors a wasted-looking punk leaned, waiting for his turn on one of the simulators. The front of his T-shirt read: *The Nintendo Generation.* There were track marks beneath the tattoos on his arms. As Norris left the arcade for the warm, darkening streets, he realised that there were now kids who could not remember a time before video. What on earth did they think about as they pounded those machines?

Change For The Sky Master

The first picture is drawn on a cream sheet of butcher's paper, about ten inches by fifteen, with soft, thick coloured pencils. Reds and yellows dominate against a dark blue background, striations of crimson linking the explosions of warm colour which appear, randomly it seems, across the paper. It could be a seascape, or a lunar garden. A mountain sunset, perhaps, its horizon landscaped by the contours of a child's mind.

'Hardly to be taken as a sign of abnormality,' said Miss Perry, placing the sheet on top of the stack and squaring its corners. She looked questioningly at Tennant.

'There are more.' Tennant leaned forward and ran the back of his hand across the drawing. 'You'll note a predominance of abstractions. No real figures — father, mother, house, trees. It's the same in all the others.'

'Do you really think so, Mr Tennant?' Miss Perry asked, looking at him over the top of her spectacles. 'I know art is taught very differently today — free expression being the educational watchword we must live by nowadays — but even so I would have thought you could see what the child is trying to convey in this picture.' She pointed a bony finger. 'It's a view from one of the windows. The library, perhaps. The child has no understanding of perspective, so it has drawn what it sees in the form of a grid, the grid being the field, and the yellow explosions here and here are simply the buildings either side.'

'What do you make of the big grey thing in the middle, then?' Tennant sat back, amused.

'You must remember that children see things emotionally, Mr Tennant. It could represent some small part of the landscape which the child, in favouring it, has blown up to a size which matches the importance it places upon the object.'

'Hmm.' Tennant considered this for a moment, then tilted back his chair in order to reach the drawer of the art chest behind him. He pulled out a further stack of drawings and placed them across his knees.

'Would you like to hazard a guess as to the identity of the artist? I'll give you a clue. It's a boy in my top first-year class.'

Tennant enjoyed these afternoon games with Eleanor. Her traditional approach in educational matters made him feel like a reckless experimentalist, although he had the feeling that in this school any teacher under forty was considered by the senior staff to be hardly worth talking to — particularly if they dealt with the creative arts. Eleanor had taught English here for nineteen years, and was therefore particularly wary of Tennant, whose fashionable clothes and casual attitude seemed to fly in the face of the school's conventions. Nevertheless, she enjoyed the freshness of his conversation, and Tennant suspected that her show of shock at his occasionally heretical ideas was exactly that.

'Have you some other drawings by the same boy?'

'Indeed I do. I also have my own interpretation of what they seem to show. I have, as you know, some amateur status as a psychologist — but then I also have the advantage of knowing the boy quite well.'

Miss Perry adjusted her spectacles further up her nose.

'Show me the rest of the pictures.'

They usually met under the railway bridge in the high street, a run-down patchwork quilt of an area, where takeaways jostled with junk shops and bingo parlours, their bright plastic signs vying for attention above the litter-strewn pavements.

They met below the bridge because here there was a burger stall run by a lanky Italian boy who would lean forward on the formica counter and let them have the frankfurters left from yesterday. They would cheek and tease one another with threatening roughness, but Mickey knew it was in fun, a preliminary to the main event which would take place in the long, low building next to the bridge. Today he was the first to arrive, and while he waited for the others, Bruno let him have a burger fresh from the crackling hotplate at the back of the hardboard hut.

'You 'ave a special on me today, Mickey,' he grinned. 'I 'ear you beat the Sky Master yesterday, no?'

'I just got through to Stage Three,' Mickey answered through a mouthful of burger. 'Never got that far before.'

'You get to put your name on it?'

'I always get to put my name on it.' Mickey was indignant. 'Every time — at the top. You got change?'

'You run get me ten pounds change, I give you change,' replied Bruno. This was standard procedure,

Mickey running across to the bank with a sack of greasy coins to replace them with fresh five-pound notes. In return, Bruno would give him enough change to last through the lunch hour, there being no change booth in the arcade.

David and Sam came running along the street shouting and scattering mothers with pushchairs to either side. They were thirteen and twelve years old respectively and, despite the fact that they were from another school, had become Blood Brothers with Mickey back at the beginning of the year, in a ceremony that was painful, and conducted as it was on the railway line above their heads, wonderfully dangerous. Laughing, the three boys took their leave of Bruno and headed along to the arcade.

'It was 62,000 yesterday and you need 70,000 for another missile,' Mickey was explaining.

Though just turned twelve and a good three inches shorter than either of the others, he was the leader, simply because he knew what *Sky Master* was really saying. David and Sam played *Astroblast*, *Super Mario* and sometimes *Maze Master*. Mickey only ever played one game. The others had tried it, but failed to score even one hundred apiece, such was the manual dexterity required to operate the phasors, joystick and Nova Blasts in conjunction with each other.

As they passed beneath the fizzing lightbulbs set in the cracked yellow plastic of the arcade entrance, Mickey felt the heavy warmth of the ten-pence pieces in his trouser pocket, and knew that today would be the day he would break the 70,000 barrier and hear the Master Of The Sky speak to him alone once more.

Bracing his legs and holding the palms of his hands lightly over the controls of the machine, Mickey readied himself for battle. The other two had snaked off through the arcade toward the Kickboxer machine. Mickey preferred to play without anyone watching over his shoulder. Sometimes Alf, the old caretaker, came over and stood by the machine, glaring at him with his good eye and recking of sour wine. Today he was at the back in the repair booth, tinkering with the oily trip hammers of a one-armed bandit. Mickey looked up at the glowing plastic nameplate running along the top of the machine. The words 'SKY MASTER' shone in deep-space letters against a wall of electronic fire. Mickey dropped two coins into the machine and watched as the operating instructions came rolling down on the readout. Normally he would use the joystick before him to beep over these, but today he ran through them. He did not want to lose the game because of some stupid slip up operating the phasors in a Stage Four attack.

He knew he had to break the 70,000 barrier today, because it was time to confront the Sky Master once more and find out exactly what he had in mind. Last night Mickey had prayed for strength. Actually prayed, kneeling by the side of his bed in supplication. He had prayed for the strength to break through the barrier, and for the strength to carry out the Sky Master's bidding, whatever the cost.

He began to play.

A cyclorama of space dropped onto the screen. Before this appeared a pulsing green grid, in the centre of which hung a large space vehicle. Mickey deftly wiggled the black plastic handle which allowed him to drop his first pilot into the craft and took off. To get to the end of the first barrier he would have to remove the grid. This was achieved by dropping red and yellow deep-space charges at weak points in the criss-cross laser lines. The trick was in locating the exact position of these points, and in avoiding the Trans-Galactic Empire's fighter craft, who could shoot you down with one burst of starfire. For Mickey, this was the easiest part. He watched, mesmerised as his bombs flowered across the screen, releasing electronic prisms of light which spun in his eyes and sent the shadows from his face.

The enemy's defence was shattered, the grid folding in on itself as it broke piece by piece and tumbled off into electric space. Mickey leaned forward to hear the first familiar words from the Sky Master himself, Grand Leader of the Rebel Force Sky Attack Fleet. On either side of the machine's headboard, grey plastic speakers crackled into life. Mickey's mouth dried.

'*Greetings, Attack Fleet Cadet. My commanders tell me you have broken through the enemy's first line of defence. You have earned your Junior Space Wings. If you wish to become a Full Attack Pilot for the rebel forces, you must swear loyalty and forsake all others in the quest to triumph over adversity. Will you swear?*'

'I swear,' breathed Mickey, gripping the joystick and moving it into position.

'*Then begin,*' commanded the Sky Master, just as he always did.

Mickey wiped the palms of his hands against his trousers and began the next stage of the game.

The second picture is an exuberant display of colour. Red borders yellow, overlapping in bands of fiery orange, while blocks of purple and blue build walls to the sky. The only similarity between this and the first picture is in the depiction of the grey object, now longer, fatter, filling the centre of the drawing with a confident weight, as if it were the generator of the surrounding chaos. The pencilled patterns are wild, the colours vibrant, buzzing with animation — and yet there is a sense of control, and ultimately, order.

'Nice use of colour,' commented Eleanor. 'Seems to prefer it over form.' She turned the sheet of paper sideways, then upside down.

'Well,' she said at last. 'This could be anything at all. An explosion. Heaven, even.'

'Or Hell.' Tennant sat back and folded his arms across his chest. 'The kid's twelve years three months —'

'You must stop adding the months after quoting age,' interrupted Eleanor with a wry smile. 'Everyone will know you're a teacher.'

'. . . and not particularly bright,' continued Tennant. 'He won't make the A stream next year if his first term is anything to go by. Yet while the rest of the class is drawing pterodactyls and racing cars, he's drawing this.'

'Wait, wait,' Eleanor tapped the table with her hand. 'You're obviously not telling me something about the child.'

'True,' sighed Tennant. 'His name is Michael Cates. I take him for Art every Tuesday and Thursday after lunch. At the start of term he showed an amazing talent. He seems a highly observant boy, and I could see him applying this power of observation to every picture he worked on. His sense of structure was phenomenal for his age. Then he began arriving late for lessons, and sometimes not at all. His work in all subjects became vague, abstracted . . .'

'And his parents became worried about his grades.'

'Right. They were plunging, we weren't doing our job, what was the point of a private school et cetera . . . so I was asked to keep an eye on him.'

42

'What's he like in class?' asked Eleanor, holding up the drawing once more.

'Well, he's very quiet. Unsmiling. Seems to have no obvious friends, almost as if he doesn't trust them. Shields his work while he's drawing. I don't think he gets picked on by the others. They just leave him alone. Or at least, they did until a few weeks ago.'

'Why? What happened?'

Tennant passed Eleanor another drawing.

'Here,' he said. 'Take a look at this.'

He was inside the Empire fortress, a floating arsenal consisting of coloured force blocks, each block capable of discharging lethal death rays which could destroy both his pilot and craft.

Mickey manipulated the joystick to dart skilfully between the blocks, blasting away at the enemy craft which lurked beyond them waiting to fire. He remembered the first time he had successfully fought his way clear of the fortress. He had tried to explain to his parents how it felt to soar freely through the stratosphere, far beyond the reach of enemy fire, freewheeling in space. How it felt to have faced the might of evil forces and to have triumphed. Naturally they could not understand, would not even consider it to be a real game. They thought real games were rugby and cricket. They thought real games had to be played on rock-hard earth, when freezing mists hung over the grass and the ground shook with the stampeding of battered muddy boots. Mickey remembered trying to explain that this game was real, realer than anything he was forced to play at school, that it taught him more each time he played, but he had known even as he spoke that his words were wasted.

His concentration had slipped.

An enemy fighter had dropped down from under a fortress block and blown his ship apart. Now he had only two ships left. He watched a new, bigger ship complete with pilot take its places on the screen. That was the penalty for losing one of your fleet: your craft increased in size, making it an easier target for enemy fire.

Mickey blasted away at the blocks in a frenzy. His sweat-slick hands were slipping on the joystick. His left index finger was sore from constantly pounding the phasor buttons. Then, suddenly, as if the rain-heavy clouds outside had parted to reveal a clear blue sky, he was through the fortress and back out into the frozen stillness of space. Mickey looked around, pleased with himself, but there was no one to share his triumph. David was across the room, still playing Kickboxer. Sam was leaning in the arcade entrance smoking a cigarette and betraying his inexperience with it by investing each puff with enormous indifference. Rain had begun to fall from a blackened sky. Mickey turned back to the machine waiting for the Sky Master's words to fill his head. The speakers crackled.

'*Congratulations, Attack Pilot. You have broken through the enemy fortress. You may now attack the rogue starships of the TransGalactic Empire. If you wish to become a Fleet Captain, free to roam the spaceways at your will, you must smash the enemy. But beware of spies who would prevent your success. Good Luck. Let us begin.*'

The speakers fell silent and Mickey began the third stage of the game.

The third picture is a tunnel of fire.

Jagged streaks of colour thrust crazily through the tunnel wall at random angles. In the midst of these spears of purple and blue stands the grey object, now split in two. The shards which penetrate the tunnel wall have been drawn with such ferocity that in several places the paper has been pierced through.

'Looks like a lot of anger here.' Eleanor turned over the drawing and noted the rips in its reverse side. 'Again, very little solid form. And you say that earlier in the term his drawings were highly structured. You mean realistic?'

'Very. While the rest of the class were copying characters from TV shows, he was giving me views of the High Street, his bedroom, buildings he'd seen. Then his attention seemed to wander, and ever since, he's been doing this stuff.' Tennant pinched the bridge of his nose and sighed. 'It was just after the change that we had the trouble.'

'What trouble?' Eleanor reached forward and clicked on the desk lamp. The room had darkened and rain had begun to spatter the common room windows.

'It was after lunch a few Thursdays ago. He had just finished this drawing.' Tennant tapped the picture in Eleanor's hands. 'I remember looking up and seeing a kid leaning over Michael's shoulder, probably trying to figure out what he was drawing. I looked away for a moment, there was a scream, and the next thing I saw was this kid clutching his cheek, and blood running between his fingers. Michael had apparently hit the kid with the paint-brush he was using. The end of it had been sharpened to a point, and it had punctured the kid's cheek clean through and into the gum. Michael says the kid started it, the kid says it was Michael, both deny sharpening the brush, and I was stuck with the angry parents the following evening. The head asked me not to mention the incident to a soul …' Tennant sat back in his chair.

'Typical,' snorted Eleanor. 'The man's scared of his own shadow.'

'... and I was once again reminded that my little charges are here on a fee-paying basis,' continued Tennant. Far in the distance thunder broke, causing the windows to vibrate behind his back.

'Have you met Michael's parents?' asked Eleanor.

'As it happens, yes. I've met them a couple of times now. She is cold, disinterested. Short-tempered with her husband. Michael's his kid from an earlier marriage. She seemed almost as distant as Michael. Fortyish, bit tarty, too much makeup and a funfur. Mainly interested in getting the kid home, to thump him I suspect.'

'And the father?'

'Oh, same age, flashy looking. Business exec, I should imagine. He stood there looking embarrassed while I explained the incident. Couldn't wait to get away.'

'And Michael is an only child?'

'Very much so. There doesn't seem to be any real friction in the family — just that half-hearted sort of distraction you see in so many of the kids' parents these days.'

'God, I know exactly what you mean.' Eleanor looked at her watch. 'I have a form to take in five minutes. Tell me the rest later.'

She stood and gathered up the essays she should have spent this last half-hour marking. After she had gone, Tennant turned back to the drawings spread before him. He glanced out of the window, down into the rainswept quadrangle where boys were dashing for fresh classes. He tapped his pencil against his teeth, thinking. Then he reached for the telephone.

*

The clap of thunder caused Michael to glance away from the machine to the entrance of the arcade. The streets were empty now as shoppers crowded in store doorways waiting for the downpour to lighten. It had been like this the first time the Sky Master had warned him about the spies. After the warning had come a sneak attack on his craft by a crippled alien starfighter, as if to teach him that it was time to be less trustful. Mindful of the Sky Master's advice he had stormed back to school to begin work on the new skymap, setting down the day's battle, recording each step of the space campaign. It was then that he had noticed the enemy watching ...

He forced his attention back to Stage Three. He played well, sending his ship spinning through a tunnel of fire thrown out by the enemy fleet to cover their tracks as they raced for the safety of their home planet. Mickey had been saving his Nova Blasts for this. Now he used them, sending streaks of light through the tunnel to rip it apart, ferreting out the enemy spacecraft which were lurking behind the walls of the tunnel and blowing them into space dust.

He glanced up at the score; 65,000 read the green computer letters. He had to hit 70,000 before he could break through to Stage Four. Then, at 75,000 he knew that he would once again hear the Sky Master's commands filtered from the stardepths through to these tinny little speakers in a run-down High Street arcade. The anticipation of that sound made his stomach lift and fall.

His mind had wandered. His plane was shattered in a burst of laserfire.

One craft left now, a lumbering spacecruiser with unlimited firepower that was a sitting duck for the more nimble enemy attack ships which were gathering around it. Mickey wiped his hands on his jacket and gripped the joystick tightly as the cruiser began to move forward. Mickey's ship was surrounded. He used his single remaining Nova Blast to destroy most of his attackers and ran the ship through the tunnel as fast as he could. To his amazement he made it in one, wiping the screen clean and preparing it for the fourth round. The score stood exactly where it had stood on Tuesday — at 72,000. As Mickey waited with bated breath, the screen darkened and dwindled to a single point of light. Puzzled, he looked up and around the side of the machine to see Alf, the caretaker dangling the machine's plug from his filthy fingers and grinning.

'*Beware of those who will do anything to destroy you.*' The Sky Master had warned him, and now here he was, face to face with the enemy.

Mickey turned away in fury, careful to conceal his anger from the senile old man, careful not to do anything that would reveal his true feelings. He could hear the caretaker's wheezing laugh behind him. Face achingly red, he dashed between the machines and out into the falling rain.

The fourth picture is black.

Tiny strokes of jet block a dense dark square. Each miniscule crayon mark corresponds painstakingly to the next, meeting in sharp, straight borders an inch from the edge of the paper. The effect is one of facing a wall, or a dead end. The mind is sealed, its walls unscalable.

'I thought I'd find you here,' said Tennant, lowering his lunch tray onto the table.

'How was period four?'

'Oh, hello,' said Eleanor, surprised to see the

gangling art master easing himself into the seat next to her. 'I didn't think you ate here.'

'I don't as a rule,' confided Tennant. 'I hate this food.'

'Look out there.' Eleanor pointed with her fork. 'Four hundred little monsters manage to eat it every day.'

'Michael Cates doesn't. He never appears for lunch. Hasn't ticked his name off on the register once this term.' Tennant cut into a spam fritter unenthusiastically. 'Any idea where he goes?'

'Some children prefer to buy chips, burgers, junk food. You know that.'

'All right then, let's try another tack. Take a look at this.' Tennant unrolled the black square before Eleanor. 'Michael's most recent picture. Collected from him at the end of Free Expression, if you please.'

Eleanor perused the drawing beyond her plate, munching slowly. 'Maybe he's depressed,' she offered lamely. 'I've felt like this picture sometimes. Are you sure you're not reading too much into all this?'

'I kept him behind after class, you know. Asked him if there was anything wrong. Got this wall-eyed look of indifference before he ran off. Most disconcerting. I wondered ...' Tennant waggled his fork at Eleanor. 'You don't suppose he's buying some kind of drug? It would explain a lot. The vanishing at lunchtime, the moods, the late attendances.'

'I shouldn't have thought so,' said Eleanor as she resumed eating. 'I grant you there's probably some outside influence at work. He may just be hanging out with a rough crowd. Kids from another school.'

'I'm taking him after lunch today,' said Tennant, eyeing a fried potato suspiciously. 'I think I'll try to keep him behind for a psychologically purging chat.'

He pushed his plate away and rose from the table.

'If you find out he's on drugs,' called Eleanor, 'ask him to get me some.'

The green computer numerals spun more quickly than the eye could follow. The score was leaping up a hundred units at a time. Mickey's hand guided the joystick more surely than it ever had before. The place was almost empty. The stormswept skies beyond the arcade had ensured that.

The rogue starships of the Transgalactic Empire fell.

The Citadel of the Emperor was within his reach.

The fourth stage had been attained.

The Sky Master had made Mickey a Fleet Captain.

His initials had been entered into the machine at a point no others had reached.

At the back of the arcade, in his dusty booth, littered with oily machine parts, the old caretaker sat, slumped forward on his stool, his face pressed open-mouthed against the nicotine coloured glass.

The liquid he had poured into the cheap sherry bottle on the old man's desk had been weedkiller, decanted from the thick glass bottle in his father's garden shed.

Now he was safe to travel beyond the beyond. To roam the spaceways at will.

The score rose fast. His hands blurred in movement between the controls, his eyes sparking with excitement, his body twitching and leaning into the machine with nervous energy. The danger had been averted. The Sky Master's bidding had been followed.

He had forsaken all others.

He had rid himself of spies.

He had dealt with those who would destroy him.

Now he would have an audience with the Grand Master of the Skies once more.

The speakers crackled and suddenly the Sky Master was all around.

You have done well, Fleet Captain,' spoke the voice. '*You are indeed a force to be reckoned with. You have broken into the Fourth Stage. You may now become a Commander. You may now attack the Citadel, wherein dwells the Evil Emperor. You must fight this battle alone. There will be no others guiding your actions. You must prepare to do battle unaided and unafraid ...*'

Mickey watched the light fade from the screen, heard the hiss of the speakers retreat into silence. His refuel time had expired. But it did not matter, for next time he would do battle with the Emperor himself. But before he could fly again, he had to free himself of others entirely. Free himself ... of whom? Of those who had been guiding his actions, that much was clear. The answer was obvious. The Sky Master could only have meant his parents. But how? Mickey checked his pockets for change. He had no more ten-pence pieces. He walked slowly and thoughtfully out into the rain, bringing the expanding world of the Sky Master with him. As he passed beneath the dripping railway bridge, he had an idea. The other night he had overheard his mother asking his father to replace the gas fire in their bedroom. She was frightened that one night the fire would go out while the gas tap was still open. God knows it jammed easily enough, said his mother.

It would all have to be very carefully planned, of course.

Soon the Sky Master would allow him to fly free and alone.

He would have to make sure he had enough change.

Citylink Four

For the city, the working day had ended and the evening had begun. A frantic jumble of radio stations blared from cruising cars. Strip joints, bars and pool halls flooded the sidewalks with hard white neon. There were a surprising number of women hanging around in red leather miniskirts. Some of them leaned in shop doorways, cooing softly to strangers, breaking off to watch cars pass.

Norris put down his travel bag and looked up at the crackling sign. The letters UCKY 7 buzzed back at him, neon pink against the deepening blue of the evening sky.

Despite the setbacks he had experienced in the last hour, Norris looked upon his trip as an adventure in sociology. After all, he told himself, everyone gets to see the tourist attractions, but who actually sees the *real* city on vacation? *Who'd want to*? said a voice in the back of his mind.

The man on the door of the club was at least seven feet tall and had shoulders as wide as a Cadillac. Ridiculously, he was wearing a pink ruffled shirt and a powder-blue tuxedo. He looked as if he was going to a Hawaiian wedding.

Figuring that by now he was getting quite good at this, Norris boldly approached the doorman and explained his problem. He was starting to feel as if his search for the hotel was the quest for the Holy Grail. Perhaps, like the Blues Brothers, he had been sent on a mission from God.

'Oh, yeah, I heard of this place.' The doorman tapped Norris's piece of paper with a sausage-like fore-finger. 'Supposed to be real nice.'

'Do you know where it is?' asked Norris, hoping against hope.

'It's right about here someplace, I'm sure of that. Go ask the bartender, he should know. I won't charge you entry.'

Feeling as if he could use a cold brew, Norris stepped inside the air-conditioned club. It was so dark that he fell over the carpet twice before reaching the bar. Clambering onto an impossibly high stool, he ordered a beer and took a look around. It was still early, and only a handful of red plastic booths had been filled, mostly with young women in very short skirts. The bartender was breathing into a beerglass and squeakily wiping it. Norris leaned forward across the counter.

'The gentleman on the door said you might know where this is.' He once again displayed the piece of paper. The barman set down his glass and squinted at the address.

'Yeah,' he said finally. 'That's the Central Hotel. Yeah, I know where that is. Nice place.'

'Can you tell me how to get there?'

'Sure thing.' The bartender thought for a second. 'Be easier if I draw it out for you. It's not far away. Couple of blocks is all.' He took a yellow pencil stub from a counter glass, drew on a napkin and passed it to

53

Norris. 'Out of here, left, onto the next block, left at the corner, a couple hundred yards down on your right.'

'Thank you,' said Norris. 'Thank you very much.'

'No problem.' He returned to cleaning his glass. The muffled song on the tape deck ended and the place lapsed into dead silence. Norris sniffed the icy air.

'There's a funny smell in here,' he said. 'Damp.'

'Yeah,' agreed the barman. 'It's them girls. They jam up the toilets with Kleenex until they overflow. We put down so much bleach you can smell it on the street. And them, you know' — he made a gesture in the air — 'them disinfectant cakes. The speed they disappear, I figure the rats are using them as breath fresheners.' He leaned forward, beckoning confidentially to Norris.

'You know, this used to be a class joint. We had a live band, cigarette girls, the works. Then it was a fag disco. At the end of the evening we used to find guys chained to the john. Then it was a soul joint. We couldn't figure out why we got so crowded until we noticed guys taping packets of dope underneath the tables, using the place as a drop point. Now it's just a regular old nightclub, and we spend our time stopping the hookers from giving blowjobs round the back of the stage. I tell you' — he sighed and leaned on the bar — 'it's a long way from Glenn Miller.'

'Perry, it's Marsha. We'll be at The Zoo later. The table's booked for nine thirty. Come along if you want or we'll see you later at Abe's. Love you.'

CLICK.

'Hello? I hate these damned things. Perry, it's Michael. Give me a ring when you get home. It doesn't matter how late. Just call me. I *hate* these things.'

CLICK.

'Perry! Perry! You there? Shut up, you guys, I'm trying to … Perry, we're over at Don's and there's this party to celebrate … what are we (indistinct) … Yeah, it's Human Rights Day in Equatorial Guinea and Constitution Day in Thailand so that seems like a good enough … (indistinct) What? Oh yeah, Diane says to call her.'

CLICK.

'This is Josie. You're never in, do you know that? Did you get my message last night? Where were you? I waited over an hour. Look, I'm not going to sit by the phone waiting for you to call, OK? I'm going over to Abe's tonight if you want to catch me. Bye.'

CLICK.

'Perry, this is Michael again. Listen, I'm really …'

CLICK.

Consuela had ironed his socks again. Maybe it was a

Mexican tradition. The place had looked as if Hurricane Betsy had passed through on a drink binge four hours ago, and was now spotless. Consuela was a gem. Maybe he should pay her more. He cut a line of coke on the mahogany dresser, snorted it, wiped his forefinger over his gums, wiped the mirror and stood it back in place. His image turned to face him. His eyes were dark and tired. He looked waxy and unhealthy. Time for a trip to the tanning parlour. His skin had a faint sheen of sweat on it, but the room was cool. Some days he felt he was losing the edge on his looks. Today was one of those days. It would be dark in a couple of hours. Artificial light was kinder. It had been a long week. A lot of partying over the bank holiday, and not a lot of sleep. After forty-eight hours straight through, he'd still had to drop a quaalude to take a nap. He was too wired, too much of the time. He'd have to learn to relax more.

Perry reset the answering machine. It was unusual for Michael to call twice the same day. Perry and Michael had been to school together, had sat next to each other in class for seven whole years, and yet now seemed to have nothing in common. Michael was studious and quiet, hated crowds and noise. Hardly the ideal companion for someone like Perry. He made a mental note to call Michael in the morning.

Now, what had he been doing before stopping to check his messages? Hadn't he been picking out a jacket for tonight? Perry wondered if he was having another memory lapse. It was the oddest thing, but twice this week he'd stopped dead in the street, unable to remember where he was heading, or why. Perry thought hard. He looked across the bedroom, blinds still locked shut from yesterday or the day before. No wonder the ficus died. He'd ask Consuela to look out

for a silk one. Unopened letters lay fanned across the
duvet cover. That was it, he had been about to check
his mail. The envelopes yielded restaurant bills,
computerised credit card expenditure forms, thank-
you notes for a party given last Saturday, details of the
winter fashion previews, a gallery opening and an
invitation which read:

SERAGLIO
The Ultimate Opening Night Party
For The Ultimate Party Club.
Saturday November 17th 1986
11 St James's Street London W1
Doors open 10 p.m.
Please bring this invitation with you

Today's date was Friday, November 16th.

'Nobody *I* know, darling. As much as one *abhors* the
mention of anything so sordid as money, does it say
how much it is to get in?'

'No mention on the card. Perhaps the invitation
gets you in for free.'

'I hardly think so, Perry. When was the last time you
got something for nothing? I mean, apart from something you had to remove with antibiotics.'

'Well, what are you doing tomorrow night?'

'I *was* planning on changing the colour of my hair. It
said magenta on the box, but this is much nearer
mauve, I swear. Do you think I should have my nose
bobbed?'

'How you manage to turn the conversation back to
your looks every time is beyond me, Diane. I thought
you'd already had your nose bobbed.'

'Don't be a bitch, Perry. That was Paula. She was

having her eyes lifted and thought What The Hell? That girl doesn't have a single feature left in its original place. She daren't stop smiling for a second. My other line's flashing, I must go. Why don't you come around and pick me up at nine, there's a dear.'

Perry had a coffee for pep and a joint to mellow out. And two aspirins, as an afterthought. He turned the invitation card over. SERAGLIO. Sounded as if it might be full of Arabs. He wondered who the owners were, and why he hadn't read or heard of this place opening up. Not that it really mattered, because he knew he would be there tomorrow night when it opened. He always was.

The evening passed in the smoke-hazed basement of a Fulham Road restaurant, where the interesting legs descending the iron-runged ladder had turned out to be Josie's, and therefore less sexually stimulating than if they had belonged to a stranger. Josie joined the table, and came along with them to Abe's, and then to a new club in Bayswater called The Palace. Perry took some speed, and snorted a couple of lines in the bathroom. Someone mentioned that Michael had been in looking for him.

The next morning, Josie had left by the time he awoke. He looked terrible and felt worse. On Saturday afternoon he went for a sauna and a sunray treatment. By early evening he was ready to face another long Saturday night. He had forgotten to turn on his answering machine, and he'd forgotten to call Michael. He tried now. No answer. From six until eight he lay on the bed eating pizza and watching old videotapes on fast-forward.

Perry shaved and showered, smoked a joint, drank a couple of glasses of wine.

The telephone rang, but he switched it into the answering machine and turned off the volume. Diane walked in just as he was knotting his tie.

'I thought I was coming to pick you up.'

'You were, but Sarah picked up this funny little croupier last night and has turned the lounge into a den of fornication. Poor dear, she has absolutely no sense of discrimination. It never pays to dabble with tradespeople.' Diane brushed the hair out of her eyes. Thick blue-black sideburns curled around almost to her nose.

'What do you think? Give me one of those, there's a dear.'

She hitched up her skirt and gave a twirl. Beads clattered and swung. She took a joint from Perry's hand and pulled heavily on it, blowing the smoke to the ceiling.

'Are you feeling OK? I must say you look a little tired and …' a pause while she held back a cough, 'a little wasted, if you don't mind my saying so.'

'I'm fine,' Perry answered irritably as he slipped on his shoes. 'Come on, let's get out of here.'

Seated in the car, Perry loosened the collar of his shirt. His neck felt sore and chafed, probably as a result of his sunray treatment. They drove to a bar in Covent Garden and collected some friends before making their way to St James's Street. Leo, a model, Sammy, an actor, Lynda, who did nothing, and a strange, silent girl who was introduced as Lotte, or at least something which sounded like it.

The entrance to the club was small and bathed in crimson. Its exterior was deserted, but once they had passed beyond the entrance desk they heard the muffled thump of music filtered from the tall mirrored doors enclosed in the far walls. Perry's shoes sank into plush redness as he peered ahead into shafts of light and dark. Before him, black-clad waitresses stood before lounging guests, mutely awaiting their instructions.

'Pretty place,' said Diane as she checked her hair once more in her pocket mirror. Perry was walking ahead, checking things out, obviously impressed. He gestured about himself.

'Pretty's right. Like the carnival in *Pinocchio*, with more subtle lighting.'

'I never saw *Pinocchio*.' Diane slid her mirror away and looked up.

'Read, darling, not "saw". Come on then, I'll buy you a gin.' Perry grabbed her hand.

The bar counter lay before them, spotless and white, almost surgical in appearance. The barmen were of vaguely Eastern extract, and slipped silently between the frosted columns behind the counter shaking cocktails and dispensing change trays. Perry pulled himself free of the crush at the bar and handed Diane her drink.

'It's damned hot in here.' He wrenched open his collar and slid the back of his hand across his forehead. 'Why on earth have they got the heating on?'

'Perry, darling, you must be feverish ... it's positively freezing. Look!' Goosebumps extended from Diane's shoulder to the mouth of her glove.

High above them, the word SERAGLIO shone in pulsing red neon, brushing heads and shoulders with seductive light. Cigarette smoke turned slowly in swathes towards the dark of the ceiling.

'Don! Don! Over here!' Diane was waving her arm above her head and pointing downward.

'Perry! Hey, you missed a great party last night. Diane.' Don bussed Diane on one cheek, then the other. Don was tall, black skinned and black leather

62

clad. His hair was slicked back into shiny loose curls and woven with beads. He appeared to have several people with him, although the insouciance of their introductions belied their acquaintance with anyone in the room. Champagne appeared, along with fresh glasses. The group insinuated itself through the crowds and up to the tall mirrored doors set into the walls beyond the bar. In front of one of them stood a bouncer of such sinister aspect that Perry involuntarily took a pace back.

'Come on, let's go through to the dance floor.' Diane was tugging at his sleeve. As they moved forward, the bouncer lightly pushed back the enormous glass doors with his palm and waited for them to pass through. Perry found it hard to take his eyes from the glistening dark features of the man's face.

The dancefloor was vast and filled. An unrecognisable dance mix pounded from banks of speakers imprisoned in a chromium trellis. The temperature had jumped at least twenty degrees. Many of the dancers had removed their shirts, their frenzied gyrations spinning them through kaleidoscopes of light. Don and his friends moved onto the dance floor as lasers criss-crossed beams and planes of red and blue, erupting into flowers of brilliance whenever cigarette smoke drifted into them. The girl called Lotte crossed to Perry's side.

'I love this song — let's dance!' She pulled at his arm.

'No, I want to wait a while.' He shook his sleeve free and stepped back from the floor. Over by the side table Diane stood tapping long artificial nails on the side of a glass. She weaved in the direction of the bar.

'Let's get another drink.' She led the way. At the bar she ferretted into her bag, withdrew a vial and slipped it to Perry.

'You can do it at the bar, no one will notice. The spoon's attached.' He nodded and ducked his head, snorting once, twice. His nostrils stung immediately.

'What are you cutting that with?' Perry rubbed the sides of his nose. 'Christ!'

The music changed. Videoscreens were lowered. Something was being projected, he could not decipher the images from this angle of the room. Other people came and joined them, hurling fragments of conversation over the pounding music. Perry removed his tie, rolling it up and slipping it into his jacket pocket. His shirt was soaked in sweat. Pulling some napkins from the bar, he undid his top three buttons and mopped up. Diane took his jacket. He was wiping the top of his neck, watching Diane fold the jacket over her arm very slowly, first one sleeve and then the other. His eyes moved from the jacket, upward along her sleeve, to the spikes of her hair and to the glint of chrome from the bar counter, to the black-suited barman polishing a glass. Perry watched him sliding his cloth around and around the glass. As it passed the rim, there was a glitter of light which splintered through to his eyes, penetrating, he felt, to the very depth of his optic nerves. The barman was staring at him and smiling, his lips conveying silent mirth, his eyes revealing none. Perry wrenched away his gaze.

'Heard a word I've been saying. Are you all right?' Diane asked, her brow furrowed.

'Yeah, fine. Come on, let's go and dance.'

'Half a hit, that can't do you any harm.'

'Acid always leaves me wasted the next morning.'

'So what are you rushing to get up for tomorrow, hey?'

Don pressed the tiny white slip onto Perry's tongue.

Across the room a singer appeared up on the stage, and launched into a fast song which sent everyone onto the dance floor. Perry found himself in a sea of bodies swelling towards the front of the stage. He felt suffocated, unable to move. Shoving his way out of the crowd, he emerged at the edge of the dance floor in a burning sweat and dropped down onto a chair against the back wall. Lotte, Don and Lynda emerged to join him after the last song. When a waiter appeared with a tray of drinks, Perry paid. He looked up into the face beyond the lip of the tray, into the blank eyes, and felt the room shift. Now Diane was in the corner, whispering and laughing with Don. She caught his eye, came over and touched his shoulder.

'Can I have the keys to the car, Perry? I won't be a minute.'

'Sure, here.' Perry shook his keys loose from the lining of his jacket pocket.

The music pounded on around him. An androgynous electronic voice sang the word 'sex' over and over again. Perry turned around on his seat to face the dance floor — and found himself facing Josie. Her hair was plastered flat on her forehead. She looked sad and pale. Perry was confused.

'Josie, where have you …'

'Perry, it's Michael …'

'Been meaning to call …'

'Perry, he's killed himself.'

'What? What are you talking about?' he said stupidly.

'This morning. He jumped out of a window. He's dead.'

Perry stared. The room shifted once more.

Josie talked on, but he could not hear her. He could see her lips moving, but the damned electronic sex-sound just hammered over her words. He felt sick.

'Got to go the bathroom ...' Perry staggered to his feet.

Under cold white globes set into the ceramic tiles of the toilet he splashed his face with water, and the rocking of the room slowly subsided to stillness. He carefully rebuttoned his shirt and combed his hair, then walked back into the heat of the night club.

'She was here a minute ago. I was talking to her!'

'Don't shout at me, Perry. I'm not deaf!' Diane swilled down the last of her glass and passed him back his car keys.

'She was here. She said something about Michael.'

'Drugs, Perry, drugs. You must have been hallucinating.' Don wagged his fingers in front of Perry's face. 'None of us have seen Josie since yesterday.'

'You are so tense, Perry. Really,' said Diane. 'Let me give you a massage.'

'I know I'm tense. Do you have a 'lude on you?' Perry held out his hand.

'Oh no you don't,' warned Diane. 'Not if you're driving back.'

'I'll leave the car here, I promise.'

'Well ...' Diane looked unsure. 'All right. But only take a half, OK?'

'The man's a walking pharmacy!' Sammy laughed and moved off to the bar with Lotte.

'All right, don't make a big deal out of it. I just slipped.'

'You hit the deck with a bang, darling, never mind "slipped". Let's see your back. Turn around.'

Diane pulled at the back of his jacket. Perry had been on the dance floor. One moment he had felt fine,

66

then the room shifted again and he had lost his footing.

'I'm great, honestly. Just get me a beer, would you?' His mouth was dry and sore, his throat stinging from having to shout all the time. 'I'll come with you, give you a hand.' He felt the back of his jacket. Stitches had torn along a seam. His spine was tender, a bruise swelling. He stood behind Diane as she joked with a waiter. Beyond her shoulder the bar mirrors threw back distorted flashes from the dance floor. He looked up slowly. Sheets of polished metal probably, not glass at all, not the way they twisted and stretched his reflected form. The mirrors made him look almost inhuman, blurring out his hairline, darkening and cracking his skin, sinking his eyes back to flat red dots until it seemed ...

'Diane, do I look all right to you?' He touched his hands to his face.

'A tad less than your usual stunning self, I must say.' Diane's smile faded. 'How do you feel?'

'I don't know.' He accepted the drink from her and walked away from the bar. 'Do I look ... different?'

'Perry, I really haven't a clue as to what you're on about. You look a little, well, tired.' She gestured at the ceiling. 'Not that one can see a thing under these lights.'

The music changed tempo. Dazzling beams of red trapped his eyes and seared his brain. As the beat of the music grew faster, revolving lights flicked up onto a huge mirrored ball and hurled shards of colour to the corners of the room. He covered his eyes with his hands. With his skin prickling and the bile rising in his throat he turned and stumbled to the bathroom once more, the beer glass dropping from his hand with a bang. Back in the coolness of the tiled room he bowed his head over the sink and tried to be ill, but nothing would come. The edges of the basin were hard and icy against his palms. He could feel perspiration trickling into his ears. His throat felt as if it were on fire. He tore at the collar of his shirt, sending the buttons skittering over the floor. The bathroom appeared to be filled with mist. He could barely make out the outline of his body through the condensation on the mirror. Scrubbing the glass with his sleeve, he stared in disbelief at what he saw.

His eyes appeared to be filled with cataracts, his skin waxy and grey. Overhead, the globe light buzzed and flickered. The room tipped. The image in the mirror changed as rivulets of water ran down. The buzzing of the light moved inside his head.

He fell back from the sink to the floor, cracking his head against the wastepipe behind. Clutching the basin before him, Perry hauled himself onto his feet and ran an exploratory hand above the nape of his neck. His skin was numb and burning. He squinted hard at the mirror again. The back of his neck was wet and warm.

Outside, somebody was trying to get into the bathroom. He must have locked the door. He took his hand from his neck and looked at it. The fingers were red. He brought them up to his face and raked the flesh of his cheeks, looking into the mirror which seemed to show the skin of his face peeling and flaking in glistening grey flakes under his nails.

'Hallucinating again ... I just have to maintain,' he thought feverishly. 'Get fresh air. Get ...' A streak of pain cut along the side of his head, through his throat, spearing his chest and shoulders. Now he grabbed his head and screamed, the sound reverberating from the metal fittings around him. He withdrew hands which held hair and skin and blood, forcing himself to look up into the mirror.

Through watery smears of condensation he barely recognised his form, a shapeless red and grey mass topped with a bloody knot of hair. He clutched at his face once more, the skin seeming to move beneath his hands. The sink below was filling with skin and bloody liquid. He coughed hard, then harder. Something sinewy entered his throat, then his mouth. His cough fell to a guttural barking deep within.

Now his arms burned. Frenzied, he scratched at the backs of his hands until they were raw but for the band of skin beneath his Rolex. As he clawed at his arms, the pain burned away to a deep fierce fire, glowing inside his chest. He tore off the remains of his shirt and dug his clogged nails into the skin beneath.

'Why don't you go and look for him?' Diane shouted into Don's ear. 'He might have passed out on the john or something.'

Don obediently loped off across the thinning dance floor. Diane looked at her watch. It was nearly three thirty. She picked up her marguerita. The ice in it had melted, the salt smearing down the side of the glass. She looked at it distastefully and pushed it to the far side of the table.

Don reappeared at her side.

'He's not in there. Must have gone home.' Don's eyes moved with the dancers as he talked.

'The bastard's probably on the make again. He'd hate not scoring on his first trip to somewhere new,' said Diane sourly. She noticed that Don's gaze had twisted away in the direction of the washrooms. 'What is it?'

'Well, it looks as if there was quite a fight in there

earlier.' He looked at Diane. 'You know, blood and stuff. You think Perry was in a fight?'

'He's a lover, not a fighter. He could talk his way out of any situation.' Diane stood up. 'Come on, give me a ride to your place.'

Don stood and linked his arm in hers and together they pushed their way out of the room.

'I like this place,' said Diane. 'It's got a friendly atmosphere.' She turned to Don. 'We'll have to come here again.'

CLICK.

'Perry, where *are* you? I've been trying to get hold of you for days. If you don't want to see me just say so, but pick up a telephone to do it, OK? This is Josie again, and *you* can call *me*, because I'm giving up.'

CLICK.

'Perry, this is Abe. I've got some primo stuff here waiting to be enjoyed, so come on over. You like, you buy. Take care of yourself.'

CLICK.

'Perry, it's Marsha. I suppose you heard about Michael. Wasn't it terrible? I guess you're feeling low, so call me in a few days. Bye.'

CLICK.

'Perry, Diane again. Where the hell are you? I came around, didn't you see my note? I'm sorry about Michael. How did you know about him? I'll call you tomorrow.'

CLICK.

The message machine records and records. Soon it will reach the end of the tape. Soon it will be dark. Behind the machine is the bedroom wall. Beyond that, another apartment, wherein more city dwellers ready themselves for the night ahead. And further beyond is the well of the building, a square dark hole filled with staves of wood, rubble and trash. In a corner of the well is a triangle of hardboard, warped by fungus and soaked in the evening rain.

Beneath the hardboard lies a ramp of corrugated iron, crusted with rust and filthy growths of mould and dirt. Below this are a number of dented sticky paint pots, strung together on a length of rope. Inside one of the pots is a piece of rancid hamburger. A rat approaches, raising itself on its back legs to pause and sniff the air. It moves on, scurrying from pot to pot, peering over the rim of each until it discovers the pungent meat. Gingerly, it enters the pot. As soon as it does so, it senses danger. Now its feet are stuck fast in the paint. Frantically it bangs from side to side trying to free itself, squealing with fear as the rope is released and the pots fall together with a clatter.

There is a heavy movement in the darkness of the corner. Dimly, a shape appears. A scaly shambling thing approaches, half covered in rags, blank red eyes flickering about itself. Suddenly it leaps upon the pots with animal febricity, tearing at one and then another until it discovers the fat, paint-smeared rat cowering from its grasp. Bony claws pull at the sticky wriggling meal with a grunt of satisfaction. Deep within the scaly wetness, intelligence sparks. A half-thought flickers, trying to make a joke about the advantages of tinned food, but it is fleeting. The concentration of its efforts

71

turns to the fulfilment of a far more basic need.

Later it will try to find a new place in which to forage. Perhaps tomorrow it will try once more to face the daylight. In time it will adapt. One thing it knows for sure. Perry's in Seraglio forever.

Marsha raised the wine glass by a delicate stem and swilled it gently, listening to the ice cubes as they clinked.

'You never told me,' she said as she watched the ice. 'What is it exactly that Perry does for a living?'

Diane thought for a moment before reaching for her glass.

'Oh,' she said nonchalantly, 'he's Something in the City.'

Citylink Five

'Hey, Sherlock! You in the fancy dress! You looking for some fun?' The girl, all of nineteen, was dressed in a Madonna outfit, a silver corset fitted with breast-cones. Norris stopped in mid-stride and stared at her. Until now, the closest he had ever been to holding a conversation with a prostitute was having lunch with an advertising executive. Madonna beckoned.

'You look kinda lost.'

'If you're looking for Moriarty, honey, I think he's dead,' laughed another girl standing in the doorway of a martial arts shop.

'You buying or just browsing, Mister?' Up close, Madonna's face was a lot older than it had seemed from a distance, which made her more like twenty. She reached out a long white arm and grabbed Norris by the waistband of his trousers. Norris, in turn, let out a squeak of surprise.

'It's kinda dead tonight. What say we go back to your hotel and liven things up a little?'

'Er, that's just it,' began Norris. 'I haven't checked into my hotel yet. I'm having a little trouble finding it.'

'That's a new one.' Madonna turned to her friend and they exchanged private smiles. 'I'll tell you what.

73

I'll do a deal with you because I love your accent. Special offer, two for one?' Her other arm slid snake-like around his waist. She ran long red nails down the zip of his trousers. Norris's palms were sweating. For a fleeting moment he considered her offer until a warning light flicked on in his head.

'Uh, you're very attractive,' he mumbled, 'but I have to be getting along.' He pulled himself free with difficulty and readjusted his trousers.

'Okay, sweetie, but think about it. If you get lonesome in the night we'll still be here. DeeDee's the name. Remember the motto: *Rolls Royce quality at K-Mart prices.*'

'It's true,' said her friend. 'It's tattooed on her ass.'

'Thank you,' said Norris. 'I'll try to remember that.'

'And have a good vacation!' The girls high-fived each other and laughed. Norris headed down the street with the napkin in his hand. When he reached the next intersection, he suddenly had a complete mental blank about the direction he was supposed to take. Unfortunately, the bartender had failed to mark his instructions with street names. The map could be any one of four ways up. Norris angrily folded his original scrap of paper inside the napkin and pushed it into his jacket pocket. It was then that he discovered his wallet was missing.

He had taken it out to pay for his beer. Thinking back, he remembered feeling the leather in his pocket when he walked over to talk to the young lady ...

Norris turned around and started back toward the martial arts store.

Not only had his wallet vanished. So had Madonna.

74

Tigertooth

As he crunched across the snow-crusted wasteground at the end of the street, he began to dread the thought of the evening ahead. He almost wished that he'd never started the business, and then remembered the money it generated, nearly enough to pay the mortgage at the end of each month. His heel cracked an ice puddle, which promptly filled with a crescent of muddy water. Sleet fell slightly, angling over the rooftops to form a fine film on the cars parked in rows up ahead.

Tonight, Conway estimated, would take at least six hours, even using three machines at once. It probably meant that Karen would become bored with waiting, and would retire early with a book, petulant and fractious. He squinted at his watch. Just ten past four, and it was already night. In the deepening gloom the streetlamps had failed to come on, and the snow all around appeared softly luminous.

As he turned into his street, Conway shifted the weight of his briefcase over to his left hand, feeling for his latchkey with his right. The case, a cheaply made 'Executive' affair of cracking black leather, was permanently weighted with the documents of his daily employment. Tonight though, it was made heavier by the blank tapes, six of them, ready to be filled with sex and horror.

Apart from anything else, it was so bloody boring. The films were all much of a muchness, shot on a shoestring budget, ineptly edited and poorly dubbed, populated with razor-wielding maniacs and huge-breasted starlets, laughable monsters and plywood sets. Why then should there be such an enormous demand for them? Why should people want to pay so much for these fourth generation softcore excursions into a world where every woman was pouting and available, and every man was a silently sexual dynamo? Many of the films were Italian and Mexican, smuggled into the country and transferred onto blank tapes by colourless men in respectable terraced houses across the city.

It depressed Conway to consider that he was forced to supplement his meagre salary in this fashion, and that he was having to take an increasing amount of this illegal work just to keep himself out of debt. He had always had big plans for himself and Karen, but these had been compromised away by ever-growing gas bills and rentals payments, car repairs and housekeeping expenses. Conway felt old and exhausted at thirty-eight, unable to keep pace with the city around him. His hair was greying, his shoulders were bowing under the pressure. He longed to move to the country, yet was financially unable to do so. These days, the only thing that kept the nervous tremors of old at bay was the gentle touch of Karen, his wife, smoothing away the fears and anxieties for one more evening. It was Karen who talked him down and set him to rights with her simple, logical way of seeing things. And it was he who would be forced to ignore her again this evening, as he set up the machines to transfer copies of 'Bloodsucking Maniacs' and 'Graveyard Tramps' for the delectation of a jaded public.

His gloved hand rested on the front gate. Before him the snow lay undisturbed on the garden path. Karen couldn't be home yet. Sometimes, towards the end of term, she stayed on at the college grading papers. Conway was aware that she hated this evening work of his, hated the sheer seediness of it, and was thankful that she had stayed behind. His shoes disturbed the fresh snow. Conway fitted his doorkey into the lock, and even as he turned it he knew that something was amiss. His stomach tightened, his step faltered. He pushed the door wide and stood back, his mouth drying.

Before him in the hallway a cup lay on its side. Ahead of it, a puddle of coffee was slowly absorbing into the nap of the rug. He stepped over the threshold and snapped on the hall lamp. At the foot of the stairs lay a pile of clothing. Further over, a glass ornament — a unicorn — was spread in pieces. Not again, he began to think. Not again. As he moved forward, glass crunched beneath his shoes. He turned into the lounge and saw the shattered television from the light of the hallway, the explosions of plaster where the cords of the video machines had been ripped from the wall, the ripped open sofa cushions, the bootmarks high on the wallpaper, as if someone had stamped and kicked in the room like a mule in a stable. Dropping his briefcase, Conway ran upstairs, passing the flung contents of Karen's dressing table drawers, passing the smashed-in door of the bathroom, the shards of the full length standing mirror. The money, the money, the money, the phrase ran around inside his head, unstoppable. The bedroom was wrecked, sheets torn off, wardrobe kicked in, broken perfume bottles flooding the little room with a sickly mixture of spices.

Sure enough, the strongbox was gone from its hiding place at the back of the wardrobe. The bedside lamp lay shattered on the floor. Conway crouched down and looked beneath the bed. There was the strongbox, its lid buckled in two, the trays within twisted and bare. Over a thousand pounds had gone. All of the undeclared profit Conway had made from this illicit work of his, gone. He sat halfway in darkness on the edge of the bed, his head in his hands, his mind blind to all logical thought, his heart raging and banging with anger.

After a few minutes he rose and returned downstairs. Karen's jewellery box lay on its side, open and empty. It occurred to Conway to begin an inventory of stolen goods. The money — already noted — three videocassette recorders, a radio, six master copies of films, luridly jacketted tape boxes which had been stacked on the machines … what else? There had to have been two of them to have shifted this lot, thought Conway. Either that, or the burglar had driven here. He walked back into the lounge and looked around. What else was missing? Jewellery, cassette deck, Sony Walkman …

Sleet drifted in through a smashed window in the kitchen, down onto a bootprint which marred the countertop below. Conway pressed the light switch, and looked up to find the bulb broken in its socket. He made himself a cup of instant coffee, his fingers plastering prints everywhere, and sat down on the floor with it, thinking.

This was the third time they'd been burgled in just over a year. Not just burgled — vandalised. What could he tell the police this time? What could he put down on the insurance claim forms that they would believe? Details of items stolen: three videorecorders for use in home piracy operation. Whoever had burgled him had known exactly what he was doing. After all, wasn't that what it was all about these days, specialisation? Wallets were for picking on crowded tube station platforms, graphic equalisers could be obtained from underground car parks, videos could be stolen from homes, good portable computers came from small offices.

There was no point in calling the police. They would just send a man to fingerprint the place and add the crime to their statistics. The only thing they could do which would be of any use would be to send someone over to clear up the mess. His thoughts leapt to Karen. He had an image of her tossing back her curled red hair as she fitted the key to the lock and swung back the front door … At least he could be thankful that she hadn't discovered the break-in this time. Conway walked back out into the hall and located the plastic pocket torch he kept behind the gas meter. Clicking its beam over the kitchen, he noticed a wad of black plastic trashbags pulled from their place beneath the sink. How convenient, he thought. We even provided him with something to gather his new belongings in. The beam swept beyond to the back door, which rested ajar. Unable to climb back out of the window with his swag, Conway's marauder had taken an easier way out, across the garden and over the back wall to the safety of the wasteground beyond, where he had presumably parked. Conway thought, he must have waited until it was dark. I could only have missed him by minutes. The coffee spilt in the hall hadn't had time to soak in.

He walked further out into the garden, shining the torch as he went. The bootprints caught in its light led to the end wall, sure enough, where two large bushes had been smashed to the ground as the thief had scrambled over with his sack. And here, just where the base of the wall met the flower-bed, was a surprise. A crumpled jacket, thin blue nylon, cheap, smeared with dirt and sporting one torn sleeve. Conway picked it up and let it turn in the light of the torch. He felt in one pocket, then the other — and struck gold.

It was a plastic wallet of the cheapest kind, and inside was a five pound note, a cinema ticket stub, a bill from a record shop in Oxford Street, the remains of what Conway presumed was a joint … and a tube season card, complete with name, address, and even a small photograph, obviously taken in a station booth. The torchlight glittered on the heat-sealed plastic surface of the pass. Conway stared at it.

NAME: DAVID LOGAN
ADDRESS: 228, WOLFE HOUSE, TRAFALGAR ESTATE, N7.
AGE: 19 YRS 4 MTHS

His breath was frosting in the night air, but Conway's face was sheened in sweat. He ran back indoors, dropping the jacket into the snow, slamming his ribs on the bannister post as he turned up the stairs.

He found it in a small cardboard box behind the wardrobe. The blade was thin and fine, but long and very deadly looking. Karen had confiscated it from a student long ago, and had confined it to the depths of darkness behind the wardrobe, too disturbing for display, too well crafted to throw away. Conway's heartbeat subsided into a more regular pulse now. He knew what he was going to do.

He did not think that he would ever be able to use the knife, but he felt sure that he would do everything short of actually pressing it into the boy's flesh. He studied the photograph carefully, the rage within him growing again. The picture showed a sallow, long-faced youth with deep set eyes. His hair was cropped to the point of invisibility, and a smudged blue spiderweb of tattoos extended from his right ear to the top of his shirt collar. Around his neck hung a silver chain, and in the centre of the chain was a clasp holding an animal tooth of some kind. Everything about the boy looked grubby, damped down, makeshift. His face was the face of a thousand other kids, his attitude one of insolence and dissatisfaction. Only the chain and the tooth looked expensive. Well finished. Stolen.

Conway strode out to the car with the boy's face filling his brain. It was a face which said I Want What You Have, a face which said Where's My Share? Conway sat in the car, his coat pulled about him, his breath clouding the windscreen. The glove box light illuminated the opened A-Z. He ran the plastic travel pass across the maze of printed streets, stopping when it reached the words 'Trafalgar Estate'. A fifteen-minute drive, if that. He snapped the book shut and threw it onto the back seat. Then he started the car's engine and slowly slithered the vehicle away from the kerb. Tonight, thought Conway, someone was going to get Their Share. Tonight, David Logan, This Is Your Life.

Pulling the car over into a rubbish strewn cul-de-sac at the edge of the estate, Conway consulted the map once more. The knife rested unsheathed in his overcoat pocket, its tip wrapped in Kleenex. As he left the car his resolve started to weaken. Perhaps he should turn around now, go home and call the police, he wondered. Further along the road two children were prising the windscreen wipers from a derelict car. Most of the streetlamps were shattered. Many were hung with old tyres. Beyond stood eight or nine vast blocks of flats, spaced like dominoes, their walls peppered with small squares of light. The few bare trees which surrounded the first block Conway reached had been stripped and scored back to the bark. A large white sign read MONTGOMERY HOUSE beneath dense, indecipherable graffiti. A scrawled-over map of the estate proved Wolfe House to be the second block along. It suddenly occurred to Conway that the boy might live at home. He had no contingency plan to allow for this situation; indeed, he had no particular plan in any event. He knew that he wanted to find the lad and frighten him badly, hopefully enough to hand back his belongings. And if things turned nasty, there was the knife — but Conway could not allow himself to think about that.

When he reached the entrance to Wolfe House he was surprised to find the building largely derelict. Plywood boards had been nailed onto the doors and window frames of the flats on the ground floor. The lift was broken, its door jammed open, its ceiling lightless. Conway climbed the stairs to the first floor, then the second, and found the corridors strewn with old newspapers, the windows nailed shut, the doors barred with wooden beams and sheets of corrugated iron.

On the fourth floor he found the address he was looking for. Here a few apartments had remained unbarred, but no lights showed. In the stairwell a single dim bulb fizzed fitfully from behind a metal grill. Conway wished he had brought the torch with him. He left the pool of light at the top of the stairs and walked into the open corridor. At this height the wind hit the pebbledashed terrace wall and blew over into the walkway with icy force. The metal numbers had fallen from the door of 228 and had been replaced with felt-tip figures. The bell did not work, so Conway hammered on the door with his fist. The hollow banging echoed in the recesses of the hallway, but no sound came from within. Conway bent down and pushed back the letterbox flap. Inside was mere blackness. It looked as if no one had been up here for a long while. Half disappointed, half relieved, Conway stood again and thought. Slowly he walked beyond the door to the opaquely patterned kitchen window, dark within, and peered through, cupping his hands around his eyes.

'Oy, what the fuck do you want?'

Conway started and turned. Framed in the stairwell was a boy of about fourteen, thin as a spindle and hopelessly underdressed for the freezing night air. His voice was flat and disinterested, his body immobile against the central pillar of the stairway.

'I'm looking for David Logan,' called Conway, pointing to the door. 'He lives here, doesn't he?'

'You a friend of his, then?' The boys hands were thrust deep into his flimsy jacket, his face an unhealthy white. He must be frozen, thought Conway.

'Yes, I am actually,' he said as the boy moved nearer. 'I was supposed to see him this evening, but he doesn't appear to be in.'

The boy watched him carefully. Conway felt in his overcoat pocket and produced a crumpled packet of cigarettes.

'Smoke?' The boy took one silently, waiting while Conway fumbled for a light.

'You don't know where I could find him, do you?'

The boy tilted back his head and blew smoke into the gloom. If he had heard, he gave no acknowledgement of having done so. Conway drew on his cigarette and wondered what on earth to say next. He had a sudden thought and felt in his coat pocket once more.

'You see,' he said, stepping forward towards the boy. 'I have something of his that I want to return.' He held up the thin wallet in the light of the stairwell. 'It's David's. He left it at my house, and as I was passing I thought I'd come and return it.'

'I'll give it to him,' said the boy, thrusting out his hand. Conway withdrew the wallet.

'No, I want to give it to him personally. How do I know you'll return it?'

The boy seemed to understand the logic in this and dropped his outstretched hand.

'He's over the pub. I just left him there five minutes ago.' The boy looked far too young to ever be allowed in a pub.

'Which one?'

'The Edward ... over there, see?' The boy walked to the edge of the balcony and was pointing to a lone building which stood about a quarter of a mile away with lights blazing all around it. The pub stood alone at the edge of a barren building site, an oasis of hospitality in a field of rubble-strewn desolation.

'He'll be in there all night if you wanna go over. I just come back. I live 'ere. Downstairs, wi' me Mum.' The boy turned to go.

'Thanks,' called Conway. 'I'll go over and see him.'

'You shouldn't hang around here,' called the kid as he ran off down the stairs. 'It ain't safe!' His footsteps echoed for a few moments, then he was gone, and the only sound remaining was the lifting and falling of crumpled newspapers along the windswept corridors of stone.

Conway stood on tiptoe as he slipped the knife under the catch of the kitchen window. The blade easily lifted the metal arm from its peg, and the frame shifted inwards. Although the panel was not big enough to enter through, it allowed Conway to slide in his arm and reach the catch to the main window. In another thirty seconds he found himself sitting on top of the kitchen counter in the darkness. Carefully he lowered himself onto the tiled floor and crossed into the hallway, feeling for a lightswitch as he went. The light revealed a cheaply decorated but presentably kept hallway, florally papered and hung with a red plastic lampshade. Further along were stacks of cardboard boxes, some of them four and five feet high.

Conway entered the lounge. The room was an Aladdin's Cave of stolen goods. Again, boxes of every size were stacked in the corners. Some of them contained videorecorders, others were filled with radios and personal stereos, pocket computers, watches, cameras and other microchip paraphernalia. On a coffee table Conway found his video boxes, and in an armchair, thrown carelessly onto a pile of similar devices, was a digital alarm clock which belonged to him. He was standing staring at the contents of the armchair when he heard a thump at the front door. For a second his heart stopped dead, then he ran on tiptoe into the hall and listened. The wind had blown half of a cardboard box up against the door, and was raising and dropping it mournfully against the wood.

Sweating with relief, Conway headed back along the hall and opened another door. It was the boy's bedroom, again piled high with boxes, all of them labelled PANASONIC, HITACHI or SONY. At the end of an unmade bed, a bundled blue candlewick bedspread yielded a pile of mudstained clothes. The far wall was a mosaic of old photographs, mostly of attractive women. Conway drew closer, puzzled. There were pictures taken with many different cameras here, and faces from many different families. The only connection between them seemed to be the general desirability of the women. A few of the shots were pornographic. Conway's eyes travelled across the patchwork of pictures until he came to the newly tacked up photograph of Karen. The shock of seeing her face here was immense, and once again the anger rose within him. It was not enough that the boy had taken those things which belonged to him, he had touched something deeper, more private and personal than any technological timesaver or toy. He had tampered with a memory. The photograph showed a younger, happier Karen, laughing into the sky, her auburn hair blown across her face. He remembered every detail of the day it was taken. He thought of her now, the laughter lines deepening with each new problem they had to face, the smile rare to form, the eyes tired with the effort of having to work and worry. He was still thinking of her as he rummaged beneath the sink, still remembering her touch, her smell, as he poured the turpentine from the bottle over the floor and splashed it against the wall. He snatched down the photograph before soaking the bed and thrust it into his jacket pocket. Fumes swirled through the pokey, cluttered bedroom as he pulled open the cupboards and splashed them with the liquid. When the bottle was empty he slung it onto the floor and ransacked the kitchen until he found a squeezy bottle filled with liquid paraffin.

Conway squirted it up to the ceiling, along the hallway and through the kitchen, over threadbare carpets and across the top of the television.

Then he returned to the bedroom and plucked a matchbox from the dripping bedside table. As he flicked the burning match onto the bed, the sudden burst of heat threw him back out of the room. Flames shot across the floor straight to the walls. The photographs on the wall at the end of the room began to buckle and ignite. His last sight of the bedroom was a hundred pairs of shining eyes staring sightlessly at the inferno, laughing faces below mops of hair, glossy, curled, cropped, but always red ...

Conway made it to the front door with seconds to spare. The flames had raced ahead to the kitchen and were even now catching the curtains, climbing the wall. Behind him a lightbulb popped and there was a renewed roar as he opened the front door and fresh air poured into the hall. He ran now, slipping on the concrete stairs, galloping down them three at a time, and out along the ground corridor past the shapes of desperate shadowy figures. He sat behind the wheel of the car shaking, hands blackened and trembling, heart pounding. He reeked of smoke and paraffin. He let his head fall onto the top of the steering wheel, and as he did so Karen's photograph slipped from his pocket and onto the floor. He wanted badly to be sick. He could not make his mind work, and yet something ... there was something in the back of his mind demanding attention. He could hear it but not see it. Gradually his breathing returned to normal. The boy. The boy had seen him and talked to him. But it did not matter, the child was obviously a little thief in the making. He'd keep quiet. And even if he didn't, so what? No, he was safe there. Something else. He started the car. Best to get out of this area. In the distance he could see a small fiery patch flickering in the wall of the second domino. No one appeared to have raised an alarm yet. He pulled out of the cul-de-sac and back into the deserted High Street. He drove slowly and deliberately, concentrating on every turn and signal, but something was pulling his concentration away. Conway looked at his watch and suddenly he knew what it was.

The boy had been lying. Conway had arrived home at ten past four. Twenty minutes in the house. A fifteen-minute drive. Three quarters of an hour here. 'David Logan' could not have been left behind in the pub. It was now only twenty-five minutes to six. The boy had wanted to protect him, but he was young. He did not realise that around here the pubs only opened at 5.30. Logan was somewhere else, yet he'd been home to dump Conway's belongings. He'd pinned up the photograph. He'd changed his clothes. He'd gone back out, seen the boy and told him where he was going. Conway's fist closed around the travel pass and he knew. The car slid around the corner of the road, shot through the lights as they turned red. He pulled into the street where he lived at forty miles an hour, and nearly lost control of the car as he brought it to an angled standstill.

The house lights were blazing. The front gate was open. As Conway ran up the path he noted the prints in the snow — his own footsteps, going in and coming out, Karen's small-heeled boots going in, another large flat bootprint going in.

The front door was ajar. On the top snow-covered step lay the silver chain, snapped in mid-link. At the end of it lay the tiger tooth.

Logan had reached home, thrown down the plastic sacks, pinned up the picture ... and missed his jacket. His wallet. His identity card.

Conway was ready for the smashed furniture and the broken crockery. He was ready for the scratch marks on the hallway walls, the splintered lock on the bedroom door. After all, hadn't all the women in Tigertooth's pictures been redheads?

He kicked open the door and stepped into the bedroom.

The one thing he hadn't been ready for was all the blood.

Citylink Six

'Long legs, nice ones, kinda looks like Madonna? That the one?'

'Yes, it sounds like her.'

'Well, you better go report your credit cards missing, 'cause you ain't ever gonna get your wallet back. DeeDee acts like she's a hooker, but she ain't.' Much to Norris's disgust, the burly man started laughing. It was so un-English. At least the people at home saved their contempt until you were out of the room.

'She's a thief, man. She comes on like a hooker to get up close. Everyone around here knows that.'

'Well, I'm not from around here,' said Norris indignantly.

'No shit, Sherlock.' He began to laugh again.

The bouncer on the door of the Go-Go-Gal Bar & Grill had beckoned Norris over after watching him walking up and down the street in total confusion. The entrance to the bar was wreathed in fizzing red light-bulbs. It made the UCKY 7 look like the Ritz. The bulbs cast a Saturnine glow over the doorman's sweat-sheened face.

'You better go find a cop,' he advised.

'I've just been looking for one.'

'They don't come around here too often. You need to go back up the street a ways.'

Norris turned around. Behind him, the sidewalks grew brighter and busier. Cabs bounced over the potholed intersection where hookers stood dipping their heads to check out passing drivers.

'Listen,' said Norris, 'I really need to get to a decent hotel.'

'Ain't no such thing in this neighbourhood.' The bouncer picked something from his teeth and flicked it at a passer-by.

Norris ignored him and continued. 'I was looking for a place called the Central, on Second Avenue, but I'm beginning to think it doesn't exist.'

'What's the intersection?' asked the bouncer.

'I don't know,' said Norris exhaustedly. 'We don't have intersections in England.'

'A limey, huh?' said the bouncer, as if that explained everything. 'Lady Di, Benny Hill, all that shit? Well, I can tell you where Second Avenue is.'

'Where?'

'You're standin' in it.'

Norris felt as if he had achieved a small victory. He stood on tiptoe, peering down the street. Darkened office buildings soared vertiginously above an endless ribbon of tarmac. 'I must be near the hotel, then,' he said hopefully. 'How long is this street?'

'It runs just about the whole length of Manhattan.' The bouncer grinned. Norris's eyes narrowed at him. He seemed to be enjoying this. One of the club's strippers came out and stood in the light-encrusted doorway. She stared at Norris's clothes, fascinated. The stripper was wearing a white mock-patent-leather imitation-fur jacket, white plastic hotpants and fake alligator-skin thigh boots.

'You wanna come in an' watch th' exotic dancers?' asked the bouncer amiably.

'No,' said Norris. 'I really think I should find a hotel and report my wallet.'

'It's a real terrific show,' he added without much conviction. 'Cassandra here has simulated action with a boa constrictor.' Cassandra leaned to one side, wiggled her fingers at Norris and snapped her gum with a bang.

'Thanks for the offer,' said Norris, drawing on his dwindling reserve of Englishness, 'but I don't really approve of strip joints.'

'This ain't a strip joint,' said Cassandra between chews. 'It's a Exotic Revue.'

Norris nodded a farewell at the bouncer, picked a direction and headed off into the deepening gloom.

'Hey!' the stripper called after him. 'Have a good vacation!'

Vanishing Acts

I suppose if you were out camping in the woods with a bunch of friends, it would be a great story to tell over the glowing embers at about two in the morning, just as the chill of the night begins to bite in. That's when I would tell it, except for three things: it's a true story, it happened to my best friend and me, and most strongly, to this day the whole thing feels fresh enough in my mind to be able to bring on my stutter if I so much as think about it.

Oh, I still get the stutter from time to time, mostly in moments of stress. It's not the only childhood legacy that I've retained, either. I'm still really weedy, thin as a beanpole, and pretty short with it, just as I was as a schoolboy. My parents always told me that when I grew up I'd be tall and strong, just like Kelvin.

They wouldn't say that now ...

Let me set the scene, as they say.

I'm now in my mid-thirties. The story I'm about to tell you happened when I was seventeen, which would make it, what, 1975 or thereabouts. It happened in winter, in London, in Soho to be precise. I'd rather not tell you exactly where in Soho for reasons I'm sure you'll understand later, but I will say that it occurred in a road running between Wardour Street and Dean Street, and that the place is still there. I walked past it about a year ago, and just looking at the entrance made my bowels turn to water.

I hate the big city. I never used to. It was our dream as schoolkids to be allowed to go there by ourselves and fool around, but our folks would never let us. We were suburban kids, Kelvin and I, and we were best friends at both junior and senior schools. I mean, we sat next to each other for about eleven years and still never ran out of things to talk about, that's how close we were. We had a lot of things in common. We were both seventeen years and nine months old when these events happened, we were both Aries, both crazy about movies, swimming, cricket, cult TV shows and mature women who looked like they could teach you a lot, all the things that seem so important when you're at school. Looking back, I suppose you could say we were also both misfits. Me with glasses and a body like a handful of pipe cleaners and hardly any friends, him big and brawny, but soft and totally unthreatening, both of us hopeless with girls, and both desperate for some kind of exciting experience with them.

I put our lack of success down to being in an all-boys school, but looking back at old photographs I have to admit we were both pretty gormless and dopey-looking, instantly identifiable as schoolkids, Kelvin with his badly cut fair hair and spots, and me with, well, everything.

The Easter holidays had just started. We were both due to leave school that summer after the 'A' level results, me to try and pursue a career in commercial art and Kelvin to join his father's advertising agency.

It was a rainy Wednesday morning, in the blackest,

gloomiest way that only England can endure sometimes, and we were walking down Ealing bloody
Broadway of all places, when Kelvin told me that he
wasn't going to be joining his father's agency after all.
I looked at him in surprise as he continued ambling
along the pavement with the rain soaking his jacket
shoulders, and asked him what he was planning to do
instead. He astounded me by saying that he was going
to join the navy, something he'd never shown the
slightest interest in before, and I got the feeling that he
wasn't too bothered about it now, beyond the obvious
fact that it would totally piss off his parents. I decided
not to say anything. I'd be losing my best friend, but I
also wouldn't have wished his parents on a dog, so
there you go.

I said I'd help him leave quietly if that was what he
wanted, and that I wouldn't say a word about it to
anyone. And the rain kept falling, and he went all quiet
and wouldn't go for coffee in the burger bar, so I
suggested going up the West End. 'Great idea,' he
said; and he got this look in his eye that I had long ago
come to recognise as meaning capital M Mischief.
'Let's go through Soho and go into all the sex
shops.'

'They'll never let us in,' I said. 'No way do we look
over twenty-one.' But we went, of course. We stopped
off at Kelvin's house first and he lent me a dry jacket.
His parents were away, thank God, and all the things
in the house that could possibly hold any interest for
us were locked away, so a trip into town seemed a
reasonable way to pass the time.

On the way there, it emerged that Kelvin's plans for
leaving were a little more developed than I'd realised.
He was talking about slipping away from home in just
a few days' time. He'd already started packing his stuff

together, and according to him all that was left to do was to head for the recruiting office, although somehow I couldn't believe it could be as simple as that. I figured he must have had a row with his parents of nuclear proportions, because he never mentioned them once in his plans. I really didn't ask too many questions, partly because I was amazed that he could even consider doing anything as totally naff as signing up with the navy. I also figured that by the weekend when his folks were due back, Kelvin would have resolved his differences with them, and would change his mind about the whole thing. I mean, at the end of the previous term he was going to become a record producer.

We got off the bus in Piccadilly and cut up into Soho. It was the first time I'd been there without my family hanging around and being a general drag, so I got the chance to have a really good look at what was going on. The first thing that struck me was that all of the strip clubs looked totally cheesy and seedy, not glamorous at all. There were these sinister looking guys sitting behind counters calling to passers-by like barkers at a carnival. Some of them sat chatting to shivering young girls who I presumed were the strippers. Kelvin kept going up to the guys on the door and asking How Much, trying to bargain with them. He was really enjoying himself, laughing, swaggering, probably feeling good about his decision, I guess.

We had a couple of pints in this grotty corner pub full of morose looking office workers eating sausages on sticks for lunch, and I told Kelvin about the history of the area. That's one of the reasons he likes me, I think, because I know a lot of useless things. I offered to buy Kelvin lunch in the restaurant part of the pub, which had huge trays of stew and shepherd's pie and bowls of lime green peas, and it was so expensive that I had to write out a cheque, just for something which looked like school dinners! So we ate and left, and went on to a sex shop, where we mucked the shop assistant about so much that she chucked us out. I kept laughing at all these ridiculous leather things. Kelvin said that if we had to use all this stuff to have sex, then the whole thing was a lot more complicated than he'd been led to believe and he was going to become a celibate. We went into another sex shop in Greek Street which seemed to specialise in whips and stuff, and got chucked out of there for laughing, too. These shops were pretty sad affairs, garish plastic places tacked onto the bottoms of nice old buildings. Quite a few had kicked-in windows which had been stuck over with tape, and huge yellow plastic signs everywhere. The buildings they were occupying still had a bit of faded elegance about them, even though they'd been carved up into offices, clubs, workshops and retailers' outlets, and it seemed that even the smallest buildings had about half a dozen different companies operating inside them. I told Kelvin that only a few years before there had been little boulangeries and cafés, and artists used to meet and exchange ideas in coffee houses, and now all these places had been turned into minicab companies and dirty book shops, and nobody cared. He said I made myself sound really old, like about thirty instead of eighteen. Then he hit me on the head and laughed.

The rain was really coming down now, and people were getting off the streets as fast as they could. There were clusters of people sheltering beneath shop awnings, and others were running past holding newspapers over their heads.

Suddenly Kelvin grabbed my arm and pulled me

into the shelter of a doorway, and the next moment, he'd vanished. The interior of the doorway was dark, but as I stepped back I could see it was the entrance to some kind of club. There were white plastic signs on either side of the doorway which said GLAMOURGIRL CLUB, then Kelvin stepped forward and waved me further in. We went down a flight of steep stairs into a gloomy hallway lit with bare red bulbs. Ahead was a large metal door with bolts all over it. At head height there was a sign similar to the ones in the entrance upstairs. The door was half open, and from inside came loud, tinny rock music. We were sort of standing there hesitating about going in, when this huge guy appeared out of nowhere and I nearly dropped dead with fright. He was about seven feet tall and looked like Magwitch from Great Expectations. Kelvin asked him how much it was to go in, and he said five pounds. Kelvin paid him the money and went to enter, but Magwitch put his arm across the door and said, that's five pounds *each*, so I pulled on Kelvin's arm meaning Let's Not Bother, but he pulled free, turned to me and grinned, then paid the Neanderthal Man another fiver from an enormous roll of notes that he pulled from his jacket pocket.

'Where did you get all that money?' I asked him once we were inside.

He told me he'd withdrawn all his savings, and it was then that I began to get the feeling that he was serious about running away. I only hoped that I could do something to change his mind before he went off and committed himself to some kind of irreversible decision. We sat down at a ricketty formica-topped table in the middle of the club and waited to order our drinks. The place was pretty indescribable, but that won't stop me: the walls were a dingy red, the same as the hallway, and so was the low ceiling. They probably got a job lot on the paint. There were spotlights all the way around the place, half of them not working, and along one wall ran a bar counter which tapered off into the gloom at one end. The whole place reeked of damp, and over it, cheap perfume, as if someone had been around with a spray trying to cover up the smell. The carpet was old, dark red and very sticky. There were about ten people in the place, mostly single men, most of them sporting the air of recently fired executives. You know, a sort of genteel middle-aged down-at-heel type — used to be in a good job, lost it along with his wife, now spends his time between job centres wandering around waiting for the pubs to open.

There were also three guys huddled together over a table in the corner who looked like they would slit your throat for a luncheon voucher. They looked Maltese or Tunisian or some damned thing, and they glanced over a couple of times. I worked hard on not catching their collective eye, concentrating on the stage ahead. This was a raised wooden platform running across the back of the club, draped in thick magenta curtains, the bottoms of which were black with damp. I was fairly revolted by the whole place but Kelvin seemed oblivious, and ordered two beers from a knackered-looking old waitress in a mini skirt. The beers arrived and I made to pay, but the waitress pointed over in the direction of the bar till, and Kelvin leaned over and told me that in places like this they ran up a tab so that you paid when you were ready to leave.

Just then the lights, what there were of them, went down and the curtains opened, and the music got really loud. The stage was wide but shallow, and sheathed in the back with — you guessed it — more magenta curtains, obviously a job lot also.

Then this girl came on.

She was black, quite pretty, with long straightened hair tied up in a knot with a red satin ribbon. She wore a glittery corset and stockings, and very high-heeled red shoes. She strutted across the stage in time to the music, which could have been anything, the speakers were distorting it so badly, and looked younger than me, although she moved like a very experienced woman. Probably one of the senior strippers had given her lessons, I thought. She pumped her body from one leg onto the other as she walked, twirling at the edge of the stage and coming back again. As she unzipped the corset and stepped out of it, Kelvin kicked me under the table. I looked across and saw his huge grin, his eyes catching the reflected light of the stage.

The girl was wearing a bra that revealed the top half of her breasts. She moved, and the breasts moved, but the bra didn't. The dynamics alone were fascinating. She bent forward at the edge of the stage and encouraged this old guy who was sitting there to unsnap the clasp at the back of her panties, then she let him pull them off. She took ages removing her stockings, then the music changed to something faster, and she removed the bra-thing and did this frenzied disco dance which was frankly pretty erotic.

After her came another woman, older and heavier, wearing thousands of layers of make-up. Kelvin caught my eye as if to say What's Your Mum Doing Up Here? and we both fell about. This one had really big thighs and long legs. She took off this long black gown to reveal a load of complicated underwear and tassels and suspenders. I thought Hello, this is going to take ages, so we ordered more drinks and by the time they arrived she was *still* only down to her bra and panties.

100

Then she reached behind the curtain and poured half a bottle of Johnson's Baby Lotion over her body and began massaging it in. As she was big and pretty wobbly all over, the effect was spectacular. Throughout the whole act her face was like stone. She seemed to be looking off to some point at the back of the room, where the wall joined the ceiling. In fact, she stared at it so much that I turned around and looked to see if there was anything there. All I could see was the moulding of the old ceiling, probably belonging to a time when the place had been a private house, before plastic had been glued over the plasterwork, before laminated plywood had been nailed over the hallways and plasterbord walls had been erected to divide up the rooms. I tried to imagine the place it had once been, with elegant scrollwork over the tiled fireplaces, and tall shuttered windows looking onto the coach-strewn street, but it was just about impossible. There had been too many people through the place, and too many changes.

Back on the stage, the woman was rubbing her crotch and gritting her teeth with her eyes screwed up tight, which either meant that she was in ecstasy or great pain, I couldn't tell which.

After this there was one more girl, a sad little thing, pale and skinny with ribs like a xylophone. She looked desperately fed up and tired, removed her clothing with a minimum of fuss and got off quick. Then the curtains closed and the music changed, and we asked for our bill.

Which was where the trouble started.

We'd had four beers between us, and the bill was twenty-five pounds.

Kelvin asked the waitress to explain, and she just referred him to the barman, another sinister type who

101

looked as if he had a summer job working at a travelling carnival. He had the words LOVE and HATE tattooed across his knuckles, and wore big chunky gold rings, about four on each hand. His eyes were really bad news, though. They peered out from an overhanging forehead, broad and flat, and I could see the icy deadness of them right the way over from where I was sitting. He had sideburns which came down to a jutting jawline. Everything about the man was too big and obvious, as if he had been designed in caricature. Long black shiny hair, flicked back onto wide shoulders — too wide for his height — and those eyes, as bright and dead as neon light. They were arguing now, Kelvin standing back from the bar, pointing over at our table, the barman immobile, watching his face.

Then Kelvin was back at the table.

'He reckons the bill is correct,' he sighed. 'Fiver a drink and an extra five pounds service charge.' He chucked the piece of paper back down onto the table and glared at it.

'Let's just pay it and get out,' I said, but even as I said it I knew we wouldn't.

'You're joking, of course,' said Kelvin, giving a little laugh. 'Let's have another.' He pointed to my empty glass. I looked at him, puzzled, as he called the waitress and ordered again. While she was away getting the drinks, he leaned across the table and called me forward.

'I just asked if we could pay by cheque. You've got your cheque book on you, haven't you?'

'Yes, but ...'

'It's simple. We have these drinks, then you write the barman out a cheque for the full amount and we cancel it first thing tomorrow at the bank.' He sat back and smiled.

'I can't do that,' I said. 'They'd probably trace the thing and come around.' I pointed over to the barman. 'He looks as if he'd come and blow my house up or something.'

'You're so green sometimes,' snorted Kelvin. 'This whole place is on the twist. It's all crooked. They can't charge prices like this legally. There won't be any comeback.'

So he talked me into it, just like everything else he'd talked me into doing over the years. We had the drinks, and then another round. Our bill was re-totalled, and I reached into an empty coat pocket to remember that I'd left my chequebook on the food counter of the pub.

By this time another show was about to start, and I was beginning to panic. Kelvin laid a hand on my arm.

'Relax,' he said. 'The pub's just around the corner. It'll just be reopening, and the barman's bound to have put it away somewhere safe. Nip out of here and get it, and I'll hang on for you. I want to check this out, see what the new batch are like.' He indicated the stage. I hesitated, worried.

'Look, just go out of here, left then left again, and the pub's facing you. Go on. If the Godfather here gets stroppy I'll just pay the bill and leave.' He patted the roll of notes in his jacket pocket.

As I left the club, the cold, relatively fresh air revitalised me. It was dark now, and still raining. Cabs were slooshing by and people were scurrying home with their heads down. As I arrived back at the pub, the landlord was just unbarring the doors. He remembered me. Luckily one of his staff had picked up the chequebook and put it behind the bar, so I thanked him, pocketed it and headed back to the club.

As I descended those steep steps again, the smell of

damp blistered my nostrils and depressed me. I wondered how many night clubs and strip joints had scarred this place over the years. The doorman waved me by, and I went inside. There were a few more old men now, and a few more secretive groups of plot-hatching wide-boys. But there, in the centre of the room at our table sat a very old man in a grey raincoat, and no Kelvin.

The old man must have just come in and sat down, because there were still droplets of rain glistening on his shoulders.

I stood over by the table for a minute, not quite sure what to do. My first thought was that Kelvin had reluctantly paid the bill and gone outside. But why? And wouldn't I have seen him standing there? He's not easy to miss ...

I went over to the bar and waited while the creepy barman finished loading the drinks onto the waitress's tray, then called him over.

'Where's the guy I was with a few minutes ago?' I asked above the sound of the endless thudding disco beat. Then I got a really good look at the barman's face. It was covered in sweat, with a kind of urgency about it that made me stare at him. Across the room, the waitress was looking back at me oddly.

'He's gone. He just left.'

The barman turned away and began to walk back to the till.

'Did he pay the bill?' I called. The barman turned and came back again, as if he had been expecting me to call him back.

'Yeah, he paid it and left.' His face was strained and dark. Then he moved forward to me and his eyes hardened. 'Go on, you can piss off out of here as well.' He gestured at the door. Being a born coward, I took his advice and left. We were both cowards, Kelvin and I. The difference was that Kelvin had the bluster and the physical presence to cover it up. I stood outside in the doorway for a few minutes, watching the rain fall. I knew Kelvin wouldn't have just made off, you see — he couldn't. I still had his doorkeys. His pockets weren't deep enough to hold them.

Eventually I decided to go back into the club. I wasn't sure what I was going to say. All I could think of was that Kelvin had perhaps gotten into a fight with them over the bill and one of them had slugged him. But where on earth was he now? Perhaps Magwitch had hit him so hard that he'd needed some kind of urgent medical attention, and had run off to get it.

When I got back into the hall, the doorman was missing, so I slipped straight back into the club. The curtains had been drawn between shows and the waitress was busily filling drink orders. But she was slipping behind the bar pouring the drinks herself. The barman had also vanished. I think that was when I began to get scared. I had an image of Kelvin with a broken nose or something. I checked the room out again. Just the same gathering of defeated businessmen, drunks and fringe members of society that there had been before, waiting for the next act to come on.

Just then the barman reappeared from a doorway by the stage and called the waitress over. They spoke urgently for a few seconds, then the waitress turned and noticed me. She did a little jump, as if I was the last person in the world she expected to see. I knew then that something was terribly wrong. As the barman slipped away again, she headed over.

'Look, sonny,' she said flatly when she had gotten close to me, 'your mate's not here. He went off home, and so should you.'

'But I was only away a few minutes,' I said. 'He wouldn't have left. Didn't he pay the bill or anything?'

'Oh, yes. He paid.' The waitress was nodding, her face in darkness. 'He wrote out a cheque, then he left.'

So she was lying. She'd heard Kelvin ask the barman if it was OK to pay by cheque, and assumed he had.

'What, you saw him pay and leave, did you?'

'Yeah. Now get out of here or you'll get me into trouble.' She turned away and made off to the bar, leaving me standing in the middle of the floor.

The rest of the evening's events passed in a kind of waking dream. I want to explain everything as it happened, clearly and simply.

As she turned away, I made off to the toilets, which were set in the wall near the back of the stage. I locked myself in a malodorous cubicle and sat down to think. I remember my hands were shaking. There were obscene graffiti all over the toilet door, and thin lines of blood marked the point where someone had shot up. All I could think was that Kelvin had started a fight. But why? He said he'd pay the bill if there was a problem. I knew he was too much of a coward to start anything serious. But he had to be somewhere on the premises, probably through the little door next to the stage. The one the barman had emerged from.

Then I realised what could have happened, and my stomach turned over.

Magwitch had seen Kelvin with the roll of banknotes when we first came in. Suppose he and the barman had done him over, and then slung him out the back? I cautiously opened the main door of the toilet and looked about. The next show was starting. The curtains had risen, and the sad-faced thin girl was back on in some kind of restraining leather outfit. The barman was back behind the bar, too. He looked as if he was taking a phonecall, his body half-turned from the stage. I only had to pass a distance of about eight feet to the stage door. I waited until he was turned away completely, then slipped across the corner. At first I couldn't get the damned thing open, until I realised that it pushed inwards. The next second, I was standing in total darkness, the music hammering on the other side of the door.

Slowly my eyes adjusted, and I could make out glimmers of light a little way off. I was standing in a damp little hallway filled with beer crates. Ahead were two doorways, one on the right and one on the left. The right one was pulled to, but I could tell through the crack that it was the girls' changing room. I could hear muffled conversation coming from within, and a cracked mirror atop a dressing table showed in the narrow gap. On the other side of the passageway, the door led to the stage and the area behind it. Cautiously I pushed it wide enough to squeeze through, and found myself at the back of the stage. Here the smell of damp was almost unbearable, the floor slick with excrescent moisture. Beer crates were piled in every available space. Beyond, through the tears in the magenta curtain, I could see the sad-faced girl bumping and grinding, the blue filters of the stage lights tinging her pointed breasts as she ran her hands over them. At the end of this backstage area was a small dark alcove. Condensation ran down the walls here, accumulated from the sweating heat of the stage. A section of mildewed curtain extended across the alcove. Above it, the glistening walls tapered off into blackness. My hand reached up to the bare overhanging lightbulb with its chain-cord, and pulled. The feeble light it threw was enough to guide my hand to the alcove curtain. I wrenched it back and stared.

Kelvin was sitting on one of those orange plastic bendy-backed chairs they have at the doctor's, his eyes half open. He had no jacket, and his face was blue-white. He was breathing shallowly, his hands crossed over his shirt as if he had a stomach ache. He didn't even raise his head to look at me. I stepped further forward.

'Kelvin, what's the matter?' I said, or something like that. 'What's wrong?' He slowly lifted his head to look at me, his eyelids heavy and his mouth half-open. He was drooling slightly, his tongue a reddish grey and lolling in his mouth.

At first I thought he was sick, that something in the drinks had poisoned him. I think I asked him if he was ill. Then I noticed that there was blood on his shirt. I moved closer to get a better look. It was hard and black, like blood and something else mixed. He was trying to speak to me. I brought down my head to his and listened. He was wheezing badly, and it was hard to hear above the pounding music.

'They took the money,' I said. 'You tried to stop them?' He nodded, almost imperceptibly. 'There was a fight?' He nodded again.

'Come on,' I said, standing up. 'Let's get out of here.' My knees touched his. I looped my arms under his and pulled as hard as I could. He winced, his face crumpling in a ball of pain. He looked as if he was dying. About three feet from us, beyond the mildewed curtain, the sad-faced girl ground her pelvis back and forth, her fingers tracing spirals on the cheeks of her blue-tinted buttocks. For a moment I caught a glimpse of her face, brightly masked in greasy make-up, like a clown, blank dead eyes staring hard ahead. I turned back. Kelvin was staring too. He grunted, and came up on his feet, his body against mine. My shirt felt suddenly hot and wet. I looked down. He had dropped his hands down. His shirt had been slashed open wide, and so had his skin. His stomach fell out against mine, part of his coiled intestine pressing against my shirt. I stepped back, dropped him and must have screamed, the shout lost in the deafening pulse of the music. I saw spots before my eyes, but didn't pass out. Kelvin had fallen back on the chair, his arms at his sides, his eyes completely turned over and blank in their sockets, the contents of his stomach protruding slightly through the slit of skin, leaking into the back of his shirt.

I turned as the door behind me opened, and there was the barman, his eyes wild. He looked at me standing there with my stained shirt, then at Kelvin's body which was sliding grotesquely from its chair, then at the floor. I looked down too. The ground was shiny with blood. It had leaked down the leg of the chair. Kelvin had bled to death. I saw the barman reach over and pick up something from the top of a crate. It was one of those small hooked carpet knives, the ones people use for getting packing boxes open. I reached up and closed my hand over the bulb above, pulling on the whole thing until it went out, and he was on me. I remember holding his arm with both hands and trying to stop it from moving towards me with the knife. For a few seconds we just stood there, both of us pushing and neither able to move. Then I felt his other arm going around the back of me, and I knew that he could kill me within seconds, just by pulling my head back and cutting my throat. He was leaning right over me, his breath on my face. That's when I slipped. My feet slid on the blood and shot from under me as I fell backwards into the alcove with the barman falling heavily on top of me. I felt a pain in my stomach, not a knife-blade pain, but a dull pressure from the handle which had slipped in his grasp and turned as he had fallen. My hands were beneath him, and I could feel that the knife had bitten deep into his groin, the curved blade entering and hooking into something hard, the pelvic bone I guessed. He was lying on me, hissing through his teeth. I tried to move a hand down. I knew the curve of the blade was hooked under the bone, I could feel it there, so I pulled. I pulled with all my might until the blade had cut deep into the bone and lodged firmly. He was half screaming, half crying now as I worked him off me. A bottle fell from a crate rocked by his writhing body, smashing and spraying us both with sour beer. I pulled myself to my feet as he tried to get onto his knees. I couldn't believe he could move at all with that thing stuck inside him. His hand reached out, and I stepped back in horror as it thrust forward through the curtain, tearing the rotted material. He staggered up and then fell, ripping his way through the material, onto the stage, the girl standing there frozen in the bitter blue light.

I had banged open the door and was back out in the darkened hallway, my chest heaving in fear and pain, wondering how the hell I was going to get out of the place in one piece, when I heard the voice.

'This way,' it said. 'Over here.'

There at the end of the passage was the figure of a woman, heavy and middle aged. Behind her a flight of stairs rose into the shadows. I followed her upward to a dark green landing and into a room. She turned on a light and revealed what looked like the remains of an old nightclub. There were a couple of once elegant armchairs, deep and winged, a pair of small tables, a mahogany bar half buried by wooden lathes and rubbled plaster. The woman was in her fifties, strongly perfumed and made up, her face heavy and sagging, her nicotine-stained fingers encrusted with gold rings. She guided me with her arm, picking her way nimbly through the rubbish, talking constantly as she did so. I must have been in shock, but I remember perfectly what she was saying as she led me through a maze of little half-demolished rooms and stairways.

'I knew it would happen again,' she said, half to me and half to herself. She had a hard, slightly cockney voice, dry with years of cigarette smoke. 'It always happens sooner or later, because this is a bad building. Always has been, right back from when the fine gentlemen held their little shows here a hundred years ago. Bringing their servant girls, making them do things they don't even do today. It ended violently, of course, how could it not? Club after club there's been since then, and always the same, death and misery ... so sad, and so unnecessary. Clip joint and sideshow and nightclub, all of them ending in evil ...'

Behind her voice I could hear another sound: growing uproar in the club. We'd reached the bottom of a flight of stairs covered in cracked brown linoleum. She let go of my arm here, her hand reaching up to touch the back of her neat grey coiffure. Ahead was a scratched steel door, for which she produced a key.

'These are violent times,' she said. 'I hate being here for them. Where evil has always lived, greed grows easily. Times like these encourage it.' She had opened the door and was holding it back for me to pass through.

'Now you must go and be thankful,' she said, and shut the door behind me. I was out on a sidestreet, out in the rain, gasping for breath and grateful to be alive. I was reeking of stale beer, smothered in blood and bile, and anyone passing me on the street would have taken me for a tramp or a madman.

I don't honestly remember how I got home. I walked a lot, I know that. I had wounded, perhaps killed someone. I couldn't go to the police.

That night I had horrific nightmares of being chased, of leaving things unfinished, I don't know. The next day I knew I had to go back.

When I arrived I found a sheet of corrugated metal over the entrance to the club. Either the cops had closed them, or they'd moved on double-quick, I'll never know.

I had lost my best friend. I had seen him die, although to this day his parents think that he ran away to sea. And someone had saved my life. Three years later, I found out who. I was working with a photographer in Soho, and he took me to a drinking club above the restaurant where we'd just had lunch.

Hung on the wall was a black and white photograph, quite old, of a group of people gathered around a bar. In the centre of the picture stood the woman I had met. She had a glass and a cigarette in one hand, and was laughing. Beneath this, taped to the glass, was a short piece of poetry. I asked the barman if he knew who the woman in the picture was.

'Oh, her,' he replied. 'One of Soho's characters. She used to run a drinking club in the forties and early fifties. Just off ...'

'I know where it was,' I interrupted. 'What was it like?'

'A bit of a legend in its own way, I imagine. The famous and the infamous drank together there.' He leaned forward confidentially. 'Rumour has it that she was the inspiration for John Betjeman's poem, the one about the nightclub hostess.'

I read the poem on the wall, and was surprised by the final line.

'I know,' said the barman. '"Old and ill and terrified and tight" doesn't seem like her when you look at the picture, does it?'

'Perhaps not then,' I said, 'but it does now.'

'It can't do,' replied the barman. 'Not now. She's dead. She was murdered in the bar back in 1957. Big scandal. Murdered for money.' The barman returned to wipe the glasses.

So this is a ghost story, I suppose.

But for me the ghost was real. My hand didn't pass through her; quite the reverse. Her arm, heavy and fleshy, had guided mine. She smelled of whisky and perfume and stale cigarette smoke.

She was right, too. It is a bad building. There's always violence there sooner or later. A little article appears in one of the tabloids, another Soho murder occurs, another disappearance is noted. The clubs come and go.

Remember I said that I walked past there about a year ago? Well, guess what the sign outside said?

'The Naughty Girl Saloon is opening here soon.'

Citylink Seven

Norris was pleased that he had at least had the sense not to keep his traveller's cheques with his wallet. He could cancel his credit cards with a few telephone calls when he reached the hotel. It was his own fault, he thought as he trudged on past darkened warehouses and shuttered shops. He should have known better than to wind up in such an area in the first place. For someone employed in town planning, he sometimes showed incredible naïvity.

He had left the clip joints and dives far behind, and now found himself walking through a darker, deader part of the city. Here the streets were broad and quiet, the sidewalks gusting with litter. Crumbling storage buildings stood beside dust-caked storefronts, but above them were the gentrified loft apartments of the artistically inclined. The whole area seemed to be standing somewhere between demolition and renovation. It could go either way.

This was probably a beautiful neighbourhood once, thought Norris. Would it ever be again? An answer to this question appeared as he passed an intersection and found himself on a block consisting entirely of rubble-strewn lots and half-destroyed facades. Half a dozen ragged-coated tramps passed bottles around an oil-drum fire, even though the evening was exceedingly warm. As Norris peered into the dark corners of the lot, he could make out many more, slumped at the base of the building's outer shell.

One of the tramps by the fire ran over to him. With the typical indecisiveness of his Libra personality, Norris remained rooted to the spot as the filthy old man flew at him.

'Hey, buddy, you got a couple of bucks to spare for an old soldier?' he whistled through broken teeth. He scratched the stubble on his cheeks and stared at Norris's clothes in wonder. 'Say, what happened to you?'

'Somebody stole my wallet,' Norris wearily replied. 'I can't give you any money.'

'Stole your wallet?' said the tramp. 'Jeez, that's terrible. You wanna hit?' He wiped the top of the Thunderbird bottle on his coat and held it out.

'No thank you,' said Norris politely. 'I just want to find the Central Hotel.'

'Oh, that's along here a couple of blocks. Or is that the Central Mission? Shit.' He pulled off his battered blue baseball cap and clawed at his greasy hair. Norris found himself scratching in sympathy.

'That's the trouble see, Mister. I can't remember nothing.'

'Why is that?'

'I'm a bum,' shrugged the tramp. 'What's to remember?'

'Well, I'm very sorry,' said Norris, 'but I have to be getting along.'

'I wasn't always a bum,' the tramp continued. 'Believe it or not, I used to have a regular job. I was a city planner! Hard to believe, huh? Now I'm living in derelict buildings. Guess City Hall got the last laugh on me.' His own laugh turned into a horrible cough.

Norris had no idea what to say. He looked at the tattered man standing lost in thought before him and tried to imagine himself in the same position. At this precise moment, it was all too easy. Suddenly the tramp brightened up, his rheumy eyes glinting.

'Say, you're welcome to stay for something to eat.'

'That's very kind of you, but really, no.' Norris swung his travel bag onto his shoulder.

'Okay, but if you change your mind, you know where we are. These guys ain't so hot on intellectual conversation, but they really know how to party.'

The tramp turned away and began picking his path across piles of shattered brickwork. His shadow danced in the light of the crackling oil-drum. He turned and shouted back to Norris.

'Some nights, when there's nobody around, we sing a cappella. It ain't the Vienna Boys Choir, but we're pretty good for bums. It's a free life.'

Norris watched until the tramp had rejoined his friends, then walked slowly away down the avenue of derelict buildings.

Her Finest Hour

Inside, the music box plays on.

It is 1946. Princess Elizabeth is nineteen years old. Houses are scarce, and the homeless are many. There are prefabs, and ration books, and Windmill Girls, and clothing coupons. Ambrose and his orchestra are on the radio. Evening dress has returned to the Savoy. In the backyards of London, there are unexploded bombs, and rubble-filled craters.

Outside, the traffic blares.

It is 1986. Queen Elizabeth is fifty-nine years old. Jobs are scarce, and the unemployed are many. There are housing projects, and apartment blocks, and areas for redevelopment, and areas of urban decay. The bombs don't need to fall to make a building come down. There are quiz shows on the television. There's bingo in the newspapers. Hotels like the Savoy are for the Americans. In the back streets of London there are gangs, and villains, and events like this one.

Emily Sutton is eighty-seven, she thinks, but she may be older than that. Her birth certificate, along with her sister Irene, went missing during the Blitz. In the twenties she was married to a man named Jack. The events of the forties changed that. Emily lives on, here in her basement flat in Cairo Road, Deptford, South London, in three rooms which have changed little since the Second World War, or the first one for the matter.

Emily is small, smaller now than she used to be. Her shoulders have rounded and her head has lowered. She spends her day watching from the window. There are no children playing outside any more, no church bells to herald a Sunday morning. There is the distant thrum of road drills and the occasional crunch of a bulldozer.

Emily moves more slowly than she used to. Her legs are thick and slow, protected with heavy support stockings and socks. Her hands are spotted and veined, the fingers no longer nimble, but still capable of holding a needle. The skin of her face is so crimped with age that it is hard to imagine her as ever having been young. For Emily, young is sixty, young is feeling the warmth in your fingers and toes, being able to hear the wireless clearly without fooling with the volume. Young is just being able to walk across a distance.

Emily is old, but she is happy. She goes out rarely. Her shopping is brought to her. She has no television and she likes it that way because she has seen and heard enough to last a lifetime. Her life has been long, but she considers it far from over. Her body is not strong. A bout of pneumonia landed her in hospital, a fall on some icy steps broke her ankle and complications set in. Now she feels better. Some aches and pains, some trouble getting to sleep, but nothing more. Her biggest problems are mostly those so common to so many old people in the city: the bitter cold of February, which this month now is. The problem of making the money last. Loneliness.

The first has been pretty much solved for her by Eileen, the social worker, who managed to get her a heater for the bedroom. Eileen is nearly sixty herself, and Emily has told her that she shouldn't be charging around in the snow and ice just for her sake, but thinks she probably needs the money, and so doesn't interfere.

The second problem hasn't been solved, but it's simply a matter of being careful. She doesn't pamper her cat like the women on the telly commercials because she doesn't put that much by a cat. She certainly doesn't prefer it to the company of a human. It's simply a pet, a creature to respect and look after in moderation. For herself, she buys the cheaper cuts of meat and cooks them beautifully,. She has always been a practical woman.

The third problem isn't quite so easy to solve. New friends are hard to come by. Old ones tend to die. Eileen calls in twice a week, and so does the delivery boy. Then there's Carrie. Carrie is her daughter. There used to be two sons, Wally and Eddie, but they are both long dead. One died gallantly trying to save his best friend in the burning sea off the coast of Gibraltar. The other, somewhat less nobly, fell onto the third rail after a Christmas party in 1949.

Emily has long been used to living alone. As she potters about the living room, winding the music box on the mantelpiece, dusting the bits and pieces on the shelves, she finds it unsurprising that in this part of her life she really has only herself for company. She has been strong enough in the past to survive the loss of her sons and her husband, and witness the gradual demise of her friends and relatives. She cares little for the daughter, Carrie, who comes to visit but itches to leave after the second cup of tea.

Now, as she sits in the dusty sunlight of the

119

window, looking out into the barren, boarded street, she thinks about her biggest problem, the shifting of time. Days and hours can be gauged by the programmes on the wireless. The years are harder to tell apart. Sometimes she goes to the shops, but the trips are painfully slow. She hears the news. She reads the new library books. The politicians come and go. The strikes rise and fall. The changing governments barely seem to cause a ripple in the still surface of her life. The shops in the High Street are owned by Asian people now. They used to be owned by the Irish, and before that the Italians, so the change means little. The boys look like girls with their hair. In the twenties she remembers the girls looked like boys. The women, they say, want equal rights, just as they did when she was a girl. The more things change, the more they stay the same. The wheel brings the same events around, just as the seasons change.

Emily makes tea and returns to the window. Beyond the glass is the slope of the front garden, littered and untended, and beyond that the deserted street. So many of the buildings have been torn down, just as they were at the start of the fifties: another cycle is beginning. And because of this cycle, Emily has days when she can no longer recall the age in which she lives. A reminding event like a birth or a death, or an anniversary for the Royal Family, will click the right time into place.

Her lack of contact with other people will cause time to slowly slip again, so that it becomes not 1986, but 1946. Often this year, for it is a memorable one. The war is over. The country has a new government, ungrateful and unforgiving for the events of the war, but one dedicated to the people. And so there will be better, more prosperous times. The Princess Elizabeth is young and radiant, and reflects the hope of her nation. In this year, Emily is forty-eight and suddenly alone. She knows that she will not remarry, but the thought does not bother her. She lives her life. The kettle boils. The cat is to be fed.

Colin and Tony are fairly accurate representatives of the new breed of violence. They are both in their late teens. They both grew up in the same borough, both left school at fourteen, both found irregular employment on the fringes of criminal society. Stealing cars for joyrides first, stealing cars for others next. A little petty larceny, a short stay in a place of minimum confinement, some minor league shoplifting with perhaps a transfer in the offing to the more profitable world of major factory heists. But these are early days. There is an interesting new sideline that it seems may develop, involving cash payments for a little intimidation. The business comes from tenants in the large blocks of flats at the back of the estate. Pakistani families have moved in, and once they're in they're like leeches on a rock. It's a sod of a job to get them out. Fifty quid in the pocket says that life will become most uncomfortable for them if they stay, though. Colin reckons lighted petrol through the letter box, but Tony's looking for something a bit more subtle. Something to do with the kids, perhaps, or the old ones. They're the bosses of the whole clan. Take them out and they all leave.

Colin and Tony are white and skinny and smartly suited. Their hair is close-cut, but not cropped. They're not skinheads, and they're a long way from being punks, who only look menacing and strange but tend to be rather shy when taken out of their element. Colin and Tony have no element. The documentaries

121

would call them 'Society's Misfits', but that's not strictly true. They're a new society. Colin and Tony don't like anything, or anybody, and it is much easier to break the law when you don't like anybody else. They're not even sure they like each other. They simply have a lot in common, like the street they are walking down the centre of as they head towards the pub at the end. The Cairo Arms, like the road, is old, brown-grey and almost deserted. They sit here over pints of bitter, saying little to each other. Colin looks up out of the smoked-glass window. Bitter sunlight illuminates the dust-filled air. He plays with a beer-mat, twisting off the corners of pressed cardboard and running trails in the spilt beer on the tabletop.

'How much money you got?'

Tony checks the pockets of his suit. He looks into his hand.

'About eight quid.'

'You know all them flats down this side?' He indicates the road beyond the pub doors.

'There's only about six of them still occupied.'

'Yeah, they're gonna pull 'em all down.'

'They won't get pulled down for years. Make good squats, they would.'

Colin takes a swig of his beer.

'You know what they say about the woman in the basement of number fourteen?'

'What?' Tony reaches for his cigarettes.

'The old cow's supposed to be loaded. Gold jewellery and stuff, stashed away since the war.'

'Who reckons?'

'Her neighbours, for a start. When they moved out they told my gran about it.'

'What, and she told you? Not exactly reliable information, is it?'

Tony blows smoke into the light. 'Anyway, she's supposed to be barmy. Thinks the war's still on.'

Colin sits back and looks at Tony.

'You got any better ideas?'

The rattle of the bell sounds along the linoleumed hallway. Emily has been dozing in an armchair by the gas fire, the tick of the mantelpiece clock faint in the back of her mind. She starts at the sound. It cannot be Eileen calling — she's at home with flu, and probably won't be calling at all this week. She is expecting no one else. As she makes her way slowly to the front door, she sees two motionless shadows against the frosted glass. She pauses for a moment, then slips on the burglar chain. She opens the door a crack. Cold air gusts in. Through the narrow space she sees two smartly dressed young men, with thin and sallow faces atop shiny grey suits. They look down at her, smiling politely.

'Yes?'

'Mrs Sutton? Mrs Emily Sutton?' The taller of the two reads from the plastic panel below the doorbell.

'Yes ...'

'My name is Mr Turner, and this is Mr ... Harris.' Colin points to his colleague, who stares at him, fascinated by the lie. 'We're from the council.' Colin feels in his jacket and produces an identity card, a blue square of paper sealed in plastic, containing a few simple statistics and a small photobooth picture of himself. All very official-looking. 'We're checking everyone in the neighbourhood to make sure that they're provided for the coming crisis.' Tony stares at Colin, amazed. His inventive mind is always planning. It never ceases to come up with something that Tony would never have thought of. Not that this is difficult in itself — Tony hardly ever thinks of anything.

'What crisis? I ... I don't understand.' Already, the old woman is confused.

'I'll explain. Do you still have your ration book, Mrs Sutton?' That throws her. It throws Tony, too. He can't imagine what Colin is getting at.

'My ration book? I don't have it any more. I don't need it ...'

Ah, so much for the old cow thinking the war's still on, thinks Tony.

'Oh, there's no need to worry at all, Mrs Sutton. I just need to see some record of your current financial situation for my records.' Colin glances warily at Tony as he says this. He cannot tell whether the old woman is all there or not.

'My what? I'm afraid I don't know anything about this.' The gap in the door starts to get narrower.

'It's actually very simple. Perhaps I could just step into the hall for a minute and explain.' Colin gives her his biggest, warmest smile. Emily frowns back at him with doubt in her eyes.

'My colleague will be happy to wait outside, I'm sure.'

The gap in the door widens once more, then slams shut.

'Shit,' says Colin under his breath. Then he hears the rattle of a chain and realises that she has closed the door in order to slip off the safety lock.

The door opens wide. Before them stands a tiny old lady in an apron and carpet slippers. She steps back, smiling, her hands nervously fiddling with the string of her apron. Colin enters the dim coolness of the hall. It smells faintly of lavender polish. He turns his back on the old woman for a second and holds up five fingers to Tony. The door closes.

'Would you like a cup of tea?' Emily gestures Colin towards the living room. Along one wall stands a bank of shelves filled with the clutter of a lifetime. Tiny china plates stand with dolls and ashtrays and miniature cats, cheap souvenirs of day-trips to the coast, taken many years ago. Faded photographs in filigree silver frames stand beside painted thimbles and small glass figurines. A black lacquered music box is silent next to a ticking brass-edged clock. The place is like a very neat and orderly junk store, he thinks. Not much of value here.

'Very nice, thank you.' He seats himself in a straight-backed chair with an embroidered cushion and waits for her to speak.

'I don't get many visitors, you know. It's nice to have someone to make tea for.' She totters off to the kitchen, a frail thing. He hears water filling the kettle, the pop of the gas stove and the clink of good china. He rises from the chair and takes a look around. On the top shelf along the wall stand three photographs in matching hinged frames. One is of a distinguished looking man in military garb, another of two young boys, remarkably similar in facial features, and a third is of an overweight girl scowling in a back garden.

'Are these pictures of your family?' he calls to the kitchen. 'On the top shelf.'

'Yes,' comes the reply. 'My daughter is still alive. She visits me sometimes.'

'Your husband ... in the army? Very handsome.'

'Yes, he was. A great war hero. He died very bravely, so they tell me.'

In the kitchen, Emily places four ginger biscuits on a plate. The cat rubs itself in a figure eight around her ankles. She turns around to take the milk from the refrigerator and jumps when she sees the tall dark frame that fills the doorway.

125

'Sorry, I didn't mean to make you jump,' says Colin. 'Thought I'd come out here to save shouting.'

'Oh, that's all right. It's just …'

'… You're not used to visitors.' Colin smiles darkly to himself.

They seat themselves in the living room. Colin stirs his tea and replaces the spoon quietly in the saucer.

'It's very simple, Mrs Sutton,' Colin begins. 'You must have heard on the news that the war is starting up again …'

'The war? No … No, I don't know anything about this. Eileen hasn't mentioned the war.'

Emily looks puzzled. She thinks hard. 'No, I'm sure she hasn't.'

'Eileen?' asks Colin sharply.

'She's from the Social Services. She comes round to make sure I'm all right. But she's off ill at the moment.'

'Well,' Colin digests this information. 'Eileen probably didn't want to worry you, but it looks as if there might be another war …'

'Who with?'

Colin gives her an old-fashioned look. 'Germany, of course.'

'Oh dear.' Emily thinks hard. How long has it been since the last one? It seems only a brief while ago. There was another war, over the sea somewhere, but she cannot exactly remember where, or who with.

'We want to make sure all the people in our area are properly provided for.' Colin's face is a picture of concern. 'Now I want you to have a look for your ration book tonight. I'll pop back tomorrow morning, and if you can't find it, I'll fill out a form which will get you a new one right away. Just in case.'

'Oh, thank you. That is a help.' Emily smiles, then her face clouds with worry. 'They won't really start

126

rationing again, will they? It seems … it seems they only just stopped …' She pulls her cotton cardigan more tightly across her thin chest.

'Better safe than sorry, Mrs S,' says Colin cheerily. He stands up to go. 'Well, I must be off,' he says. 'I don't like to keep Mr Harris waiting in he cold. Thanks for the tea.' Emily follows him out into the hallway. In the doorway he turns and looks down at the old woman.

'I'll be back tomorrow morning. Then we'll sort you out.' He flashes a smile.

'Thank you. You're very kind.' Emily opens the door for him.

Colin steps out into the sunlight and rejoins his friend, who is stamping up and down the road outside with his hands thrust deep in his pockets.

'How did it go?' he asks as soon as they have cleared the street. 'What did you get?'

'Hold out your hand,' says Colin. He drops a small gold thimble into Tony's outsretched palm. Tony holds it up in the sunlight. Engraved on the side are the words '*To Emily with love from the girls 1948*'.

'Is that all? Hardly worth the effort …' Colin gives Tony a sharp look.

'You know your trouble?' says Colin. 'You got no finesse. There's a lot more where that came from. And I know how to get it. Give us that back.' Tony hands him the thimble. Without another word he cuts away across the wasteground, leaving Tony standing on the corner, wondering what he said wrong.

'Here, wait up!' Tony runs after the retreating figure striding over the rubble. 'What's the plan then?'

Colin turns on his heel and faces the panting boy. He takes out the thimble and raises it between thumb and forefinger, suddenly smiling.

'You think she's got money hidden away?'

'Not money,' says Colin. 'Something more valuable. Something she can't put out on the shelves with her knick-knacks. Old people are all the same. They get given something nice and they don't want to use it. They put it away for "best". That's what she's done.' He turns to go.

'What do you reckon it is?'

'You be here tomorrow morning at eleven,' Colin calls back, 'and we'll find out.'

As night falls, Emily dusts the shelves and finds the thimble missing. Heartbroken, she looks for it high and low, to no avail. It was a gift from the girls of the Adelphi underground, with whom she worked in the war. She checks through the dustbin to see if it has been accidentally thrown out. Then she washes her hands and decides that a thimble is not the most important thing in the world, so she makes herself a cup of tea, and has a little cry.

Colin puts the next part of his plan into operation. He visits a joke and novelty shop in town, catching them just before they close, and has a newspaper dummied up with a false headline.

The next morning, at eleven fifteen, the doorbell rings at number fourteen, Cairo Road. Overhead, the storm clouds gather.

'Hello again, Mrs S. You remember Mr Harris, don't you? Can he come in this time? It looks like rain.'

'Why, yes, of course. Please come in.' Emily steps back from the front door to let the men pass through. Colin leads them into the living room. It has been polished since yesterday, with the knowledge that company is coming. The smell of lavender is everywhere. Emily stands before the two young men, her hands clasped over her apron. She looks up guiltily first at one face, then the other.

'I'm ever so sorry,' she says. 'I've turned the place upside down but I can't find my ration book anywhere.'

Colin looks worriedly at her as he seats himself.

'Don't worry, Mrs S. I brought along those forms I mentioned.' He pulls out two sheets of paper filled with type. 'You just hang onto them and we'll be able to issue you with the full amount of coupons any day now. Of course, things are a lot more serious, what with the official outbreak of hostilities.'

'What do you mean?' Emily frowns, trying to understand.

'Perhaps you haven't heard the news this morning?' asks Tony gently.

'No, I haven't had the wireless on,' Emily admits. Colin beckons her forward.

'The war's begun,' he says confidentially. Emily's hand flies to her mouth.

'Things have taken a grave turn,' says Tony. 'This morning's papers ...'

'The papers hold bad news.' Colin unfolds the newspaper he has had printed and lays it flat on the table. The headline reads: 'WAR DECLARED, RATION BOOKS TO BE ISSUED.' Emily reads the large type with widening eyes, and Colin quickly stows the paper away.

'But let's try to keep a brave face,' he says cheerily. 'How about a cup of tea?'

'Goodness, how rude of me,' says Emily, rising immediately and making for the kitchen. Beyond the lace curtains, the blackening clouds roll.

'By the way,' says the tall one, as he sits sipping his

tea, 'I have something for you.' He reaches into his coat pocket and — lo and behold — produces the golden thimble. 'This dropped out of my trouser cuff when I got home last night,' he says, proffering the thimble and smiling his smile. 'I thought to myself, now who could this belong to? And I remembered that I'd been here earlier. It must have fallen right into my turnup.'

He sets the thimble down on the table.

'Oh, I can't thank you enough,' says Emily. 'It's really such a little thing, but it means so much.' Tears form in the corners of her eyes.

The clock ticks on. A distant clap of thunder rattles the window pane. The young men talk of war.

'It's so worrying, the thought of fighting. And over what? Pieces of land ...' Emily shakes her head in disbelief. 'The last one ... the bombs falling ... I was very frightened, but I never said so ...' Her eyes are clear as she remembers back.

'We'll make sure you're all right,' says Tony, winking at her in a friendly, knowing way. 'When are you expecting Eileen, your social worker, back, Mrs S?'

'I'm afraid I don't know when she'll be back at all. A man called to say that she'd be away for a week ...' Emily touches her finger to her lip, trying to recall the conversation.

'Well, not to worry. We can get you temporary ration coupons. We're not supposed to give preferential treatment to anyone, but I think you're a special case.'

'No,' Emily insists. 'I'll wait my turn; it's not fair on the others.'

Colin smiles a sly smile at Tony, as if to say, See?

While Colin is helping the old lady remove the cups, Tony wanders around the living room. He hears the saucers rattle on the draining board and the murmer of conversation. He opens a small box on the top shelf, keeping his eyes on the doorway as he does so. Fishing around inside, he pulls out a small pearl chain, turning it in his fingers. This he quickly pockets. Nothing else here worth pinching, he thinks. Colin and the old lady come back into the room.

'Now we're working on getting you — and the rest of the street — issued with the appropriate books as soon as possible, but you have to fill out the form I brought with me.'

'Of course,' says Emily, apologetic that she is taking up so much of their time. 'Perhaps you could … my eyes … I haven't had my glasses changed yet.' She trails the sentence away, embarrassed by her failing faculties.

'That's quite all right,' says Colin. 'I'll give you a hand. Now then.'

He seats himself at the table, licks the end of a ballpoint pen and prepares to fill in the form for her.

'I can take care of the essential details, but there are one or two things I need to know.'

Emily sits quietly waiting, hoping that her memory can cope with these official details.

'In the event of an emergency, are you financially secure enough to survive on your own money?' Colin translates. 'Have you something put by for times like this?'

'Well, no, no I don't,' Emily begins worriedly. 'I no longer have a bank account. You see, after Jack, my husband — well, after him, I used up the money in my savings account …' She looks down at the table, her voice as tiny as a distant bird. Talking of such matters in front of virtual strangers is uncomfortable. Emily has rarely discussed such matters before.

'I'm sorry,' says Colin. 'I can't hear you. Could you speak up?'

'My husband ... when he ... left me ... he left debts. The bank was very difficult. I have a small amount in the Post Office. Some premium bonds ...' She looks as if she is going to cry.

'What else?' asks Colin curtly. 'Do you have any other way of raising money?'

'Well, er, perhaps one other way, yes.' She coughs into her fist gently, then pulls free a handkerchief from her sleeve and dabs at her mouth. Colin's eyes are black and glittering in the gathering darkness. He fidgets as he waits for her to continue.

'I have a medal case. It contains ... well, not medals, but something that my husband Jack was holding in safekeeping for a friend after the occupation of Paris. The friend never contacted us again. When Jack tried to trace the rightful owner, he found that the man had been killed along with his family in the bombing raids near the end of the war. Then Jack went and I had no way of returning the case. I feel very bad about the whole thing.'

Thunder rattles the window, nearer now. Tony reaches over and switches on the lights.

'You shouldn't feel bad, Mrs S.' says Colin. 'It's not like stealing. You tried your best. Would you like to show me the case?'

'I've never shown it to anyone since Jack ...' Doubt clouds her face. She remains seated.

'Well, it's up to you, of course.' Colin plays it close. 'But it would help us to evaluate your financial position if we saw it. Then we could get this form completed, and sent off ...'

She looks to the bedroom door, her hand touching the side of her face, the back of her hair.

'And as soon as Head Office receive the form, you get your ration book.'

That decides it. Emily stands and makes for the bedroom. As she goes, Colin stands, motioning Tony to stay where he is. She advances into the room, the young man following behind. He stands at the edge of the doorway and watches her move a chair around the bed. Slowly, painfully, she climbs up on it and reaches to the top of the huge wardrobe. She lifts down an old red metal biscuit tin, covered in dust. Colin quickly resumes his chair. He is enjoying himself now. He checks his watch. Emily enters with the biscuit tin between her tiny hands. She sits, puffing with the exertion, and slowly pulls off the lid. From within she removes the medal case. It is square and flat, a black leather envelope fastened with a brass button. A smell of mildew emanates from the tin.

Emily unclips the leather flap and pulls free a black satin board. Clipped into it are seven exquisitely carved gold medallions. These were not forged in this century — they are much older. Carved with staffs and snakes, they are inscribed in French. Elaborate scroll-work surrounds the words. The gold is soft and almost red. The medallions are linked with entwined chains. Colin begins to perspire, even though the living room is cool. He wants to touch the medallions, to run his fingers over them. And soon he will, for he knows that in just under five minutes they will be his. He may even cut Tony in, just for being here.

'They're very nice, Mrs S ...'

'Oh, please call me Emily. I feel that we're friends now.' Tony looks at Colin and grins. Colin shoots him a dangerous look back. He turns to Emily, who is already sealing away her beautiful secret in its leather pouch. The room is darker without the glow of the gold. Outside, the clouds break open and the rain begins. Colin had not counted on this. He looks at his watch. It is time to act. He prides himself on using no violence, and hopes that it will not be necessary now. Pakis and shopkeepers are one thing, but old ladies ... Emily stands and picks up the biscuit tin. As she returns to the bedroom with it, Colin calls after her.

'That's good, Emily. I'll put "Financially Secure" on this form. You could get a lot for those pieces. We'll get your ration book through in no time. And the sooner the better. The bombing could start again at any time, you know.'

Tony gives Colin a puzzled look.

'I'm doing this with no nastiness,' whispers Colin. 'You should be grateful. Listen and learn.' He smiles, pleased at his own cleverness.

Emily reappears in the doorway.

'Do you really think the war will go on?' she says.

Go on? Colin thinks fast.

'Oh, it could last for years,' he says. 'Why, on the way over here I was nearly killed ...'

'That's right,' says Tony, catching on. 'Why, if he'd have stayed on the same side of the street, he wouldn't be here now. A doodlebug, it was.' He's nodding at Colin, playing the game, understanding his intention to get her confused, thinking it's the forties again. But why? Tony thinks hard as he hears Colin talking about the bombing raids. So that she'll be confused when she reports the robbery. If she even reports it, she's so embarrassed about having the stuff. And if she talks to her social worker about the men and the war and the ration books, well, the woman will think she's being dotty again. He smiles to himself. The lad's a genius. This could set them up in the little old lady business. There must be thousands of them in this area alone,

134

trapped in their basements refusing to be rehoused ...
The sudden bang ends his train of thought. He looks
to the window. Even though Colin had been expecting
it, he sits there startled.

The old girl is clutching his arm in fear. The storm
must be right overhead now. Rain suddenly lashes the
window. Colin notices that it leaks, running water
down the lintels.

'Heavens!' cries the old woman. 'That's not the
bombing, is it?'

Another thunderclap, deafening and directly above
the house, shakes the room.

Colin jumps to his feet, grabs the old woman's hand
and pulls her up out of the chair.

'My God, it's a raid!' he shouts. 'Quick!' Emily looks
wildly about the room. Tony jumps up and stands by
her.

'Come on, Emily!' shouts Colin over another slam
of thunder. 'Into the kitchen! You'll be safe there!' He
pushes her towards the kitchen door. Tony knows that
he is expected to help at this point, but he doesn't
want to have to hurt her. Colin has said that they'll just
lock her in, take the medal case and leave, no problem.
There is a huge flash of lightning beyond the window
which stops them all in their tracks. The old lady turns
to the young men and opens her mouth, about to
speak. Suddenly she knows what she must do ... time
has fooled her once again. There seemed a gap
between the wars, a period of peace, but now Emily
knows that her memory has been playing tricks on her
again.

The war is still on. The Blitz has not ended. The
nightmare is not over. She remembers now what Jack
told her to do.

Colin pushes her towards the kitchen. He signals

Tony for a hand. Emily is lost to both of them. She is remembering Jack. Jack, who deserted the army and hid until the war was over, leaving her with the shame she will never forget, no matter how much the time slips and slides. Jack, who'd said he would come home at the end of the hostilities, who never did, who never even had the guts to confront his wife with his cowardice, so that Emily must always refer to him as having 'gone' rather than being dead. That is why, for her, the war can never end.

All he did to help her survive the bombing of London was telephone and make sure she was still alive. She remembers his advice then. What to do in a raid …

'Mr Harris, Mr Turner!' she shouts to Colin and Tony. The strength of her voice stops them both dead. 'Come with me!' She darts from their grasp, into the kitchen, and flings open the back door, releasing a wall of rain.

'What's she doing?' Tony shouts. Colin looks back, confused.

'She's got something else hidden away. Greedy cow.' His eyes glisten in the shadows of the kichen. He pushes eagerly forward with Tony following close behind. Outside in the rain, the old lady pulls at the rusty handle of a wooden door just beyond the kitchen.

'You *have* got something else!' He turns to Tony triumphantly. 'She has!'

'Yes!' calls the old woman above the storm. 'Yes! Quickly! Quickly!'

She frees the door, pulling Colin into the darkness, then grabbing Tony.

'There's room for two!' she calls. 'Save yourselves! I'm an old woman — it doesn't matter about me!' She shuts the door tight and runs back into the house as the storm rages on overhead.

In the pitch darkness, Colin steps forward and falls down a flight of slippery steps into icy water, deep and fetid. Tony lands on him, closing the water over his head. When he surfaces, he hears Tony screaming, his voice echoing from the walls.

'I can't swim! Christ, what is this?' He's splashing about in the filthy water some feet off, but Colin can't tell where.

'Shut up!' shouts Colin. He is trying to think, but the freezing liquid is quickly numbing his body. The smell is making him sick. He can feel his stomach turning over. Suddenly Tony screams again, more desperately than before, his voice rising octave by octave, as if in great pain. A flash of lightning bursts around the edges of the door, illuminating the interior of the pit for a moment, and in it Colin sees Tony writhing in the muck, howling, a rat hanging by its teeth from the flesh of his cheek. Then, he too feels the first searing bite. He threshes in the water as the warm bodies of the rats drop over his face, some biting where they land, others swimming past to the flesh of his chest.

He screams for as long as there is a tongue in his head ... which is not too long.

Emily turns on the wireless and settles into her favourite armchair. It is peaceful now. The bombing has ceased. The innocent cries of the victims caught outside when the raid started have died away. Perhaps the neighbourhood has seen the last of the bombing. Emily listens to the music and watches the hands travel around the clock. A new piece begins — Beethoven's Fifth. She sits forward, waiting for the opening chords which are the call sign of the war. She has no more fears. The present has retreated further than the past, to be recalled at some point in the future, when it is needed. She rests her head back once more, humming along with the tune as she watches the sun reappear between the clouds beyond the lace-draped window.

It is 1946.

Princess Elizabeth is nineteen years old. Houses are scarce, and the homeless are many. There are prefabs, and ration books, and Windmill Girls, and clothing coupons. In the backyards of London there are un-detonated bombs, and rubble-filled craters. And bomb shelters.

Citylink Eight

Norris stood at the bottom of the steps of the Central Hotel and growled. It was something he always did when he was angry or frustrated. He looked up again at the smart facade, the tall white marbled columns, the polished brass of the revolving doors. The hotel was everything he had hoped it would be, barring one thing. It was shut.

Once again he read the sign hanging between the entrance doors: CLOSED FOR REFURBISHMENT UNTIL NOVEMBER.

He looked around hopelessly, praying that he'd find another hotel in the area. But the streets here were quiet and residential — a far cry from the city blocks he had crossed earlier in the evening. The address had been incorrect all along. An off-duty cab driver had aimed him in the right direction.

Norris brushed back his thinning fair hair with the tips of his fingers. He'd find a call-box, call a taxi and ask to be taken to the nearest hotel in the neighbour-hood. It would be easier (and more expensive) to head for one of the big hotels bordering Central Park near Columbus Circle, but he hated the impersonality of such places. Once, when he was a child, his mother had taken him to visit a sick aunt. He remembered little of the visit except that his mother had checked them into an enormous modern hotel.

One afternoon the young Norris wandered off along one of the corridors and spent the next two hours completely lost among the identical floors of the building. It was a disturbing experience for a sensitive child, and for this reason Norris had always maintained an irrational fear of such places. He wondered if anyone else ever felt the same way ...

The Cleansing

'And how will you be paying, sir?' The reservations clerk looked up as she spoke. She looked like an air hostess with all that swept back blonde hair, the tan and the whiter-than-white smile.

'It'll be American Express,' Kent felt for his wallet and produced the green plastic card.

'I can take an imprint now, sir, if you wish to use Express Checkout.'

'What's that?'

'Simply inform us of the morning of your departure and your completed bill will be slipped under your door. Then just leave your key in the room and leave. You'll avoid time-consuming checkout lines.' The clerk smiled her widest smile yet and nearly sent Kent reeling. Like every other member of staff in his vision, she wore the peach-and-purple uniform of the Dalton Hill Hotel Group. A huge badge declared her name — Sheree — and volunteered the information that she'd be happy to help Kent anytime.

'Yes, I'll do that. That's fine.' Kent slid his credit card across the counter and watched as she filled out the tracing-paper slip. So I'll be avoiding time-consuming checkout lines, he thought, marvelling at the girl's sales patter. I'll also be avoiding any human contact when I leave. I guess that makes me less of a nuisance.

Kent turned away from the desk and looked around. The hotel foyer was a spotlit sepulchre of bad good taste, with its corporate sculptures and colour-themed relaxation areas. Peach marble-faced tiles crossed acres of floor and ran smoothly into walls containing vast purple murals of coarse woollen fibre. Orange stone statues of an indiscriminate nature and indeterminate motif surrounded an enormous low square fountain piddling peacefully in the lounge area, where mauve nylon seating units dipped between high ficus trees of suspicious artificiality. Somewhere in the background 'The Waltz Of the Toreadors', rearranged for the electric organ, featured in the Muzak programme. A few minutes ago it had been a dirgelike Mantovani version of 'C'mon Baby Light My Fire.' The counter girl returned his credit card and handed him a slim white card with holes punched in it.

'Your doorkey, sir. Just insert it into the lock and wait for the red light to turn green.'

Kent hated these pass keys. After spending a couple of days in a back pocket they always got creased and started to malfunction. Kent thanked the girl and turned to pick up his luggage. He was surprised to find all three pieces gone.

'Your luggage will be in your room when you reach it, sir,' said the clerk, smiling inanely. 'Dalton Inn Hotels welcome you and hope that you have a nice stay.'

Her speech over, she switched off the smile and returned to her computer terminal as if he had suddenly ceased to exist. Feeling as if he had just been dismissed, Kent turned and left the counter. He felt uncomfortable with no luggage to carry. He pocketed the pass key and crossed the lounge with a vague feeling of intimidation. Everything around him had been designed to soothe and relax. Everything was spotless, shiny and litter-free. Kent hated it, and decided that only in America could they make you feel threatened by the décor. But, as a hotel-stopover veteran, he had come to accept it as the people's benchmark of elegance in this country. Above the elevator bank, a mountainous chandelier of clear glass globes and long brass rods thrust down from the vaulted, pebble-dashed ceiling, making Kent feel awestruck and insignificant as he waited beneath it. The structure, he noted with amusement, was bigger than his car. The elevator arrived and Kent stepped in, checking his pass key for the room number as he did so. His suite was on the twenty-ninth floor, out of a possible forty-five. The Muzak was playing in here, too. He keyed the twenty-ninth floor button and the elevator rose. His shirt was sticking to him, his suit itchy and twisted from the flight. He couldn't wait to jump into a hot bath and soak for an hour, but realised with a sigh that he would first be expected to call the exhibition centre and inform them of his safe arrival. He hoped the maid had left the air conditioner on. Outside, on the street, it was about eighty degrees, but the humidity was unbearably high, and Kent realised that he would probably have to return to the hotel during the day and change into dry clothes. As the elevator doors opened with a ping, they revealed a vast orange mirror set in the opposite wall of the corridor, beneath which stood a purple bowl of artificial flowers. Next to this, a large plastic sign directed him to his room.

Kent reached his door and inserted the pass key into the lock. A tiny LED lit red, then green, allowing him to turn the handle and enter. Inside, the room was cool and spotless. On the bed lay a huge cardboard cutout of a coffee pot, which he presumed was a breakfast order card. The television offered a selection of cable and pay-TV channels. A card on top of the set explained that there was a special channel pointing out the whereabouts of various facilities within the hotel. Kent's luggage stood neatly in line at the foot of the bed, on peach-coloured carpet still showing the track marks of the vacuum cleaner. He loosened his tie and crossed to the window. Kent was in New Orleans, but with the exception of the view from the window, figured that he could just as well be anywhere else in the world. There was nothing he had seen in the hotel so far that could inform him of his geographical location. His room looked out high over Canal Street, the main thoroughfare of the city, and took in a panoramic view of the Mississippi dock area, the vast brown river winding sluggishly down to the edge of the French Quarter, where white paddle steamers stood waiting for tourists to board.

Kent turned from the window and caught sight of himself in the mirror. All this travelling was beginning to take its toll. At forty-five, he figured he should be in better shape than this. American businessmen seemed to take better care of themselves. They were always smartly groomed, and certainly seemed to keep their waistlines under more control. As he slipped off his jacket, Kent noticed how paunchy he had grown over the last year. His hair had greyed at the sides without managing to make him look at all distinguished. Extinguished, rather. The flights, particularly those across the Atlantic, were having a more lasting effect on him. The bags under his eyes seemed to remain a lot longer than they used to.

Kent stripped off his clinging shirt and headed for the bathroom. The guys at the exhibition centre could wait for a while. Above the sink, the brutal overhead lights made him look and feel even worse. Grey hairs were sprinkled through his moustache. The sink surround was in peach-coloured plastic, and his eyes matched it. Maybe Val was right. After this year, he should settle down in the London office and let someone younger do all the running around. Being out in the field had made him wealthier, but money wasn't everything, and he was sure that he could live without the airlines losing his luggage at regular intervals and the bellhops forever waiting to be tipped. But, he thought as he brushed his teeth, if he settled down back at home, would he ever get used to using a toilet which didn't have a 'Sanitized For Your Protection' strip across the seat?

During a luxuriously long bath, he made ample avail of the Dalton Inn Hotel Group's Own Brand soap, conditioner and shampoo. Following this, he dried off and slumped in front of the television. Channel 24, he quickly discovered, was devoted entirely to what was euphemistically referred to as Late Nite Movies. He flicked on for a moment and watched a huge-breasted blonde bouncing up and down on a skinny Italian man who was still wearing his socks. It was too early in the evening for that sort of thing. He switched to NBC for the sitcom hour, lay back and fell asleep instantly.

When he awoke, it was dark and he was hungry. Kent wished that he hadn't slept for so long. He knew this would mean that he'd wake up at five the next morning, raring to go. Realising that he had forgotten to check in with his American counterpart at the exhibition centre, he quickly punched out the number and discovered that they were not expecting him until tomorrow anyway. This suited him down to the ground, which at the moment was an uncomfortable twenty-nine floors away.

Glancing over at the digital clock set into the bedside table, he noted that it was just after seven. Outside, the lights of the cruise ships glittered as they crossed the Mississippi back and forth. New Orleans, like so many other towns across America, seemed to cater for its transients more than its residents. Tourism provided its main income, and the vast purple and peach hotel, like the other 1,200 hotels in the chain, specialised in putting the tired traveller at ease by setting him in familiar, yet impersonal surroundings. Kent hated this special kind of corporate blandness, but had to admit that the ease with which services were discreetly provided allowed him to spend more time thinking about his job. He sat on the edge of the bed, pulling on his shoes. Yes, he was totally free to sit here all night and worry about work. He shook his head. There was definitely something wrong with the profit-conscious symbiosis of the system, but he was too hungry to give a damn about it right now.

On his way to the lobby, Kent shared the elevator with about ten tiny Japanese businessmen, all of whom seemed very excited about something. But then, he thought exhaustedly, Japanese businessmen always did. The Muzak was playing 'Bridge Over Troubled Water'. In the salad bar on the ground floor, cutely named the 'Country Pantrie', Kent devoured a brightly coloured plateful of Mexican specialities, none of them tasting remotely special or Mexican. The Country Pantrie girls were a big-boned breed. Each one sported a perfectly coiffured matching hairstyle, a fixed smile and a too-short skirt in house colours which featured the dimples in her knees somewhat too prominently.

146

After signing for the meal, Kent headed back to his room to change his jacket. He had decided to take a stroll down to Jackson Square in the French Quarter, and to the river beyond. He was reasonably familiar with the town, his company having sent him here last year on a similar PR exercise. That time they had booked him into a hotel nestled beneath the freeway which had specialised in a hardy strain of cockroach undaunted by the blows Kent had rained upon its representatives with the heel of his shoe.

In the elevator on the way back down, Kent noticed that there was no thirteenth floor. The buttons in the polished brass panel before him ran from twelve to fourteen. He found it surprising that a race as practical and realistic as that of the US business executive could be superstitious, but what other explanation could there be? High on the carpeted walls of the elevator were illuminated photographic panels highlighting the two main restaurants of the hotel — 'The Southern Belle' and 'The Steamer Saloon'. Both pictures showed a girl in a low cut dress and too much make-up accepting a huge umbrella-bedecked drink from a man who looked like a surfer in a business suit.

As he passed through the lobby on his way out, Kent noticed one of the hotel staff members changing the welcome board, ready for the arrival of a new set of conference members. It read: DALTON INN HOTELS WELCOME UNITED RETAIL DEVELOPERS ASSOCIATION OF WISCONSIN. Beneath it, another message was being assembled to read: ALSO INTERNATIONAL ORTHO-PEDIC POSTURE BEDDING MEMBERS. Kent smiled to himself. Things could be worse for him after all. Outside, the night was warm and clammy, as a heat mist moved in from the river and spilled over into the streets of the old French Quarter. Here, amongst the

147

balconied colonial buildings lay a very different world from that of the main street, with its high-rise hotels and shopping malls. Here in the backstreets were the hidden courtyards and gardens of the old families. Kent turned onto Bourbon, with its strip joints and jazz bars, their neon signs shining dully through the gathering mist. He stopped in a corner bar and listened to a sweating saxophone player for a while. A few beers later, he returned to the hotel in order to ready his notes for tomorrow's round of meetings.

In the lobby, the first crowd of conference members had appeared. They were standing together surrounded by mounds of luggage, greeting their fellow members with laughter and back slapping. One of them, a huge bespectacled Texan who reminded Kent of LBJ, was talking more loudly than the rest. The plastic badge on his lapel announced him as a Retail Developer (whatever that was) named Brad. Something in his conversation made Kent stop and turn. He had heard a floor mentioned — the thirteenth — and something else that even now he could not recall. LBJ suddenly stopped laughing and turned to him. Behind the glasses were vengeful cold eyes. Kent started, a shiver passing over him as he threaded his way through their luggage. At the elevator bank he turned and looked back, uneasy without knowing why.

Just as he had predicted, Kent awoke just after five in the morning. The sun had not yet risen, but already the temperature had begun to climb sufficiently for Kent to have to switch on the air conditioning. He sat back in bed, the television bleaching a corner of the room, as a hyperactive weatherwoman revealed that today's temperature would reach the mid-eighties. While she continued to wave her arms about over high-speed satellite pictures, Kent showered and donned a light-weight suit before heading downstairs for a rubbery Country Pantrie omelette.

Over at the exhibition centre the temperature had climbed to nearly ninety degrees. The sawing and hammering of the carpenters caused voices to be raised and headaches to take grip. The morning passed in a round of efficiently organised meetings called to decide the exact running order of the upcoming trade shows Kent's company was financing. He had been sent out primarily to give advice on the running of the English market section of the show, a job he found easy and enjoyable under normal conditions. Today, however, he was uncomfortable and irritable, a migraine developing. Lunch followed with one of his West Coast counterparts, a large-framed easygoing man called Collis. Tall and tanned, his self-control was evident even in the way he ate. Kent looked dejectedly from his stack of cottage fries to the small salad Collis picked through as he spoke.

'This is a Pagan city,' he was saying. 'You should be here during Mardi Gras. Jesus Freaks on every corner screaming hellfire. Real scary.'

'I should like to see it one day,' said Kent, guiltily dipping his cottage-fried potato in a pot of ketchup. 'Where are you staying?'

'Over at the Marriot.' Collis waved the waiter over. 'It's my home from home, room's exactly the same as the one I stayed in in Tokyo. Fucking great, I love it. You wanna beer?'

'Certainly,' said Kent, painfully aware of how strange his English accent sounded.

Collis obviously did not share Kent's uneasiness about the vast impersonality of hotels. On the contrary, he seemed to relish it as an opportunity to escape from his wife and kids, and get into 'some serious fooling around' as he put it. His lack of embarrassment when it came to discussing sex, ambition or money struck Kent as being both admirable and appalling. After lunch, they attended a lengthy conference which at a quarter to eight appeared to show no sign of reaching a conclusion. Collis hissed at him from across a row of chairs, pointed to his watch and then at the back door. Quietly they slid out of the conference room and headed over to Kent's hotel for another gargantuan bland meal in the Country Pantrie.

Collis had apparently decided to deprive the women of New Orleans of his company for the evening, and proposed instead to take Kent drinking in the lesser-known bars of the French Quarter. Kent was pleased to be in the company of an American who actually enjoyed a beer, after having watched so many weird TV commercials promoting healthy alcohol-free sugarless exercise-packed lifestyles.

'I was beginning to think that nobody here drank any more,' laughed Kent as they headed towards a bar on Rampart Street.

'Ah, you don't wanna take any notice of that crap,' snarled Collis. 'Those commercials come out of California. They're all screwed up out there.'

'But I thought you lived in San Francisco.'

Collis looked at him, faltering in mid-stride.

'I do,' he said smoothly. 'But we don't consider ourselves to be part of California. LA, that's where the nuts come from.' They continued ambling along the sidewalk, their jackets over their shoulders.

'Now,' said Collis brightly. 'I'm gonna take you to a little Cajun joint where the bar staff aren't even aware that the South lost. These guys only speak French, so they'll never understand a Limey. You let me do the talking.'

And talk he did, as they perched on barstools in the warmth of a deep brown saloon, and Cajun fiddles played on the jukebox. He paused only to summon the barman in strangely accented French. He talked about the company, the Success Ethic and the Will to Win. Some of what he said seemed like brainwashed business jargon. And yet some of it made sense.

'You're English, you should know what I mean. The Freemasons — now look at them. The old guildsmen of London, created to protect what they believed in and foster that belief in others.' His eyes burned with the enthusiasm of his subject. Kent imagined that the man could be very persuasive in business. He was several years younger, that seemed certain, yet he had the assurance of someone much older and wiser.

'The whole point is,' he said, stabbing the bar with his forefinger, 'the level of success is down to you. If you don't take it, someone else will.' Kent found himself nodding and agreeing, more because of the alcohol than the force of Collis's argument.

Suddenly Collis started and looked at his watch.

'Shit,' he said. 'Gotta go. See ya tomorrow.' And he slipped from his stool and was gone. Kent was amazed that anyone could be so involved one minute, only to disappear the next. He looked at his own watch: Twelve thirty. What the hell, he'd stay for a couple more and then head back...

Kent had enormous difficulty climbing down from his stool. Outside, the fresh air revived him slightly, and he shambled his way slowly back to the hotel. As he pushed through the revolving door, he checked his watch again: One fifty. The vast, peach-marbled hallway was deserted now but for a night cleaner sliding an electric polisher back and forth in the distance. Even the Muzak had stopped, leaving the fountain to burble on in relative silence. An electronic ping announced the arrival of the elevator, and Kent stepped in as soon as the doors parted. As he reached to press the floor button his sense of balance shifted, and he fell against the panel with his palm outstretched. The elevator suddenly rose, leaving Kent's stomach behind as it did so.

From the walls around, the smiling couple having dinner beamed down benevolently. Kent keyed the correct floor just as the elevator slowed to a stop and its doors opened.

Kent's mouth fell open.

Facing him, against the corridor wall, was the usual orange mirror and purple bowl of flowers. And next to that was the plastic floor sign. It read: 13TH FLOOR.

Kent squinted first at the sign, then at the button panel beside him. The numbers still ran straight from 12 to 14. There was no 13, and yet here it was beyond the elevator doors, together with the mock colonial hall table and the plastic flowers and the standard peach-coloured wallpaper.

Intrigued, Kent stepped from the elevator. He walked over to the hall table and raised one of the two chairs framing it, placing this between the elevator doors. He wasn't sure why, but his drink-furred brain wanted to prevent the lift from moving on. He walked off along the corridor, looking for numbers on the doors, and was surprised to find a complete lack of doors, let alone numbers. The corridor ahead was straight and square and featureless. There were no rooms. Then, at a bend in the passageway, he began to hear singing of some kind — not so much singing as a rhythmic talking — and found it growing louder with each step he took. As he turned the corner he found himself walking towards a pair of large whitewood doors. The rhythm-singing was coming from within.

There was a thud behind him, and Kent spun around. Back in the main part of the corridor Kent saw that the elevator doors had toppled the chair, and were moving it out of the way as they repeatedly opened and closed. Panic cut through his drunkenness, and he ran back to the elevator, jumping inside just as the doors shut. When it reached the twenty-ninth floor, he kept his finger on the Open Doors button. What was he so scared of? He could feel the hideous thumping of his heart. Had he imagined the floor, the singing? He pressed 12 and the elevator doors closed once more.

When they opened again he found himself faced with the usual mirror, flowers, and sign: 12TH FLOOR. He tried 14. Nothing out of the ordinary there, either. Confused and annoyed, he returned to his room and drifted into a fitful sleep.

The next morning Kent awoke with a spectacular hangover. He showered and smartened himself as best as he could, but felt no better. The lobby welcome board was now greeting the Hosiery Wholesalers of Nevada. He couldn't imagine what they were doing all the way down here. His headache persisted throughout the morning meetings. The clammy warm air in the exhibition hall made matters worse. Collis came and spoke to him, making no mention of his sudden disappearance the previous night. The day passed slowly and uncomfortably. At dusk, the desk area of the hotel was once again packed with arriving conventioneers. Kent headed directly for his room. He had half begun to think that he had imagined the whole thing. So much here made him feel strange and uneasy, even the very normalness of the place. The business of the floors, the odd conversation in the lobby, the hostile look of the Texan, the behaviour of Collis ...

When he reached his room he called up the clerk on the reception desk.

'This is Mr Kent in room 2958. I have a friend staying here, on the thirteenth floor, I think ... '

'That's impossible, sir. We don't have a thirteenth floor.'

He lowered the receiver, replacing it gently in its cradle. Maybe he was just overtense. The travelling really would have to stop. Tomorrow was the last day that he would be required at the exhibition centre. He had the option of staying on for the trade show, an option he now decided not to take.

Things were out of kilter here. Even his door had refused to open earlier, the red light stubbornly refusing to change to green. He had finally gained entry by meticulously smoothing the pass key out until its creases were flattened. He made a mental note not to stick it in his back pocket any more. He took a beer from the refrigerator and returned to the telephone, sitting on the bed with a pad and pencil.

'Hello, Front Desk? This is Mr Kent in room 2958. I'm going to be checking out the day after tomorrow, so I'll be using your express check-out service. By the way,' he said, deciding to try one last time, 'I notice you don't have a thirteenth floor in this hotel. Why is that?'

'Just a minute, sir.'

There was a pause on the line. Then a man spoke.

'Standard policy in all our hotels, sir. People don't like to stay on a floor with an unlucky number. Especially in a city like this. Was there anything else?'

154

'No. No, thank you.' Kent hung up and looked down at the pad on which he'd been doddling. A crazy thought crossed his mind. He had drawn the numbers 1 and 3. He remembered falling against the button panel when he entered the elevator. Outstretching his hand on the pad before him, he looked at the fingers, then drew rings around the tips of the first and the third. Between them, he drew a 2. That's what he'd done last night. He'd pressed 1 and 3 together. At what time? He remembered it was after one ... and before three. He pulled his crumpled suit back on, shoved his room key into his back pocket, and slid on a pair of Sperry's. Then he settled down in front of the TV, through news bulletins and police dramas for nearly four hours, waiting for the appointed hour. Finally the bedside clock clicked over to 1.00 a.m. He closed the door of his room quietly as he left and headed for the elevators.

The first to arrive was full of partying conventioneers. He let it pass and collected it when it returned empty. Stepping in, he pressed the two buttons together. This time when the doors shut there was another sound, the click of a relay. His drunkenness had masked the noise before. The elevator dropped, the glowing models in their illuminated frames grinning down at Kent, symbols of health, success and beauty.

When the doors opened again, he found himself on the thirteenth floor, just as before. Without thinking, he stepped from the lift and the doors banged shut behind him. There was nothing for it now but to go forward.

Once again he found himself in the featureless corridor. At the far end a faulty light panel buzzed and flickered. He turned the corner, and now the rhythmic voices started. His hand hovered over the handle of the huge double doors. A droplet of sweat fell onto his shirt collar. Inside, the sing-song chanting grew louder. His hand closed over the handle and began to turn.

Once he had turned it as far as he could, he pushed gently against the wood. The door moved fractionally inward. Inside, it was dark. Whoever was within would see the light around the door growing as he entered ... Kent's heart was in his mouth as he opened the door wide enough to slip through.

As his eyes adjusted to the light, Kent saw that he was standing at the back of about two hundred men, assembled in a large, high-ceilinged hall. Somewhere at the front, lights flickered, and seemed to provide the only source of illumination in the room. The men were all smartly suited, and were standing to attention with their hands gathered before them. By the bowing and gentle nodding of their heads, Kent assumed that they were praying, and that he had stumbled into some private religious meeting. He was about to move back to the door when something made him stop.

The men weren't praying. They were reading aloud. He listened.

'*Success through Strength. Strength through Belief. Belief through Purity. Purity through Cleansing ...*' Kent began to feel that there was something very weird going on, but he was curious as to what.

'*Power through Unity. Unity through Obedience. Obedience through Submission. Submission through Faith. Faith through Success ...*' The pattern began again.

The man in front of Kent had heard him moving forward and turned around. Clean-shaven and smartly turned out, he could have been one of a million corporate businessmen working in the city. He wore

156

the plastic introduction badge of a conventioneer. For a moment his eyes caught Kent's and held them. Then, losing interest, they turned back to the book in his hands. Kent breathed out. Two rows in front of him was an empty chair with a book on it. Kent slipped into the space, lifted the book as surreptitiously as possible and assumed the same posture as the others around him.

The cover of the book was stamped with just two words: AMERICO. INC. The inside pages were filled with what seemed like liturgical text, with psalm-like doggerel related not to the church, but to business.

All around him, the voices droned on as if this recital had taken place a thousand times before. With a shock, he realised that the tall man two rows in front of him was the Texan who had stared after him in the hotel lobby.

Suddenly the voices stopped and a man at the front of the assembly spoke. Everyone looked up at the stage. Before them stood the platform, dimly lit by free standing spotlights. Seated on metal folding chairs at its edge were five men. A sixth stood nearby at a lectern. Kent was not entirely surprised to note that one of the five men seated was Collis.

The speaker, a typically young, smart executive, requested everyone to be seated. As he sat, Kent took a quick look around. Every member of the assembly was wearing a plastic introduction badge. All were perfect examples of the ideal American business executive.

'And so to the main business of the evening ...' The speaker's powerful voice carried to the back of the room. Nobody moved. Kent felt like he was attending a self-realisation seminar.

'We have some recently enrolled members here

with us tonight, and as this will be the first time they witness a Cleansing, I hope you will all bear with me.' The speaker turned to face the people on the platform.

'Welcome, gentlemen, to the 614th Division of Americo Incorporated. Welcome to a corporation — no, a *society* — of businessmen of America.' Here there was a spontaneous outburst of applause and cries of 'Yeah!' and 'Right!' Kent's mind reeled with the thought: Six hundred and fourteenth division?

'You know, although we have nearly a million members across the length and breadth of this great land, we are still unique. Yes, unique, for we are the *only* organisation in America to combine the Success Ethic with a Personal Belief Lifestyle — a religion, if you will.' The hall was silent now.

'United in spiritual brotherhood, sexual unity — as those of you who attended last Friday's meeting with our Sister chapter will vouch ...' There was general laughter at this. '... and joined by a common bond, a commitment to the betterment of this country, to keep it pure in body and spirit ...' Kent had already noted a complete lack of black people in the room. He looked back at the speaker. '... by keeping our sexual, physical and spiritual needs satiated within the corporation ...' The voice rose, impassioned. '... and most of all, by golly, getting out there and selling our asses off!' Laughter and applause swept the room. Kent was appalled, but joined in the applause to prevent being discovered.

'This, then, is what we believe.' Everyone bowed their heads at this.

'We believe in the creed of physical and mental selling supremacy, through sexual and spiritual self-control. Life, death, fear and strength, within the corporation. We believe in ourselves!'

'*We believe in ourselves!*' Two hundred voices joined together as one, and Kent nearly passed out. So this was what Collis was going on about. A vast organisation keeping its members tied together with the promise of sex, success and wealth. Somehow, Kent felt it was what he had subconsciously suspected about the country all along. No wonder Collis had been excited. He was about to be initiated. Cleansed.

On the stage, the initiates were being prepared.

'Now, as you know,' the speaker resumed, 'we have exciting plans for the future. Plans which involve expansion into new areas, just as our counterparts have in Japan recently. Each new division is designed to provide the best for its associates, whether they be air hostesses or company directors, shopkeepers or newspaper magnates.

'But before we can do this, before we can assure a sound future for every member, we must be sure of their loyalty. Not just job loyalty. Not just family loyalty. But a total depth of trust and commitment which will last forever.

'To do this, we ask of each member that they participate in a simple, but painful, ceremony. It is a ceremony which seals the future and assures trust. This we now ask of you new members, in the Ceremony of the Cleansing.'

As everyone rose to their feet with this cue, organ music began to play from the front of the stage. For Kent, the illusion of attending some loony revivalist meeting was complete. While preparations took place on-stage, several of the standing men changed their seats and rows in order to be near friends. Kent felt that before this they had been arranged in some kind of hierarchical order, and were now free to arrange themselves as they wished. He took the opportunity to move forward as far as he could, and gained a seat in the second row from the front. As he sat down, he turned and recognised his neighbour as being one of the cashiers from the front desk of the hotel. He prayed that he would not be recognised in turn.

On the stage ahead, about forty men had assembled to form a tiered choir, while several others noisily manipulated a large metal contraption into position. It was shaped like an X, roughly the height of a human, and at the end of each metal shaft there was a horizontal rod. At either side of the device, uniformed guards stood waiting for the first initiate to be brought forward. The speaker sat as the choir began to sing, a terrible schmaltzy hymn filling the room. It could almost have been an ad jingle, or a piece of elevator Muzak.

The first initiate, a tall, heavy-set young man in his early thirties, was brought between the flickering lights and roughly and efficiently stripped by the guards. His clothing was folded neatly and stacked by helpers, then placed in a plastic bag. Naked, the man stared straight in front and over the heads of the two hundred strong audience with no flicker of concern over any aspect of the ceremony. He was then encouraged to step onto the X, his hands gripping the rods at the top, his feet resting on the lower bars. The chant of the choir rose as a new figure appeared on the stage. He was young, around twenty, with a build of a football player. He was dressed in an outfit half business-like and half military. A small leather box was tucked beneath his arm. As the music increased in volume still further, he withdrew from the box a long, fine-bladed knife, its steel shaft catching the light and glittering like an enormous surgical scalpel.

He turned to face the initiate, and raised the knife as

160

he did so. Kent felt himself reel in the heat of the room. He wanted to turn away from the scene being enacted just yards in front, but knew he could not without revealing himself. Surely he wasn't going to …

The knife was lowered until the blade touched the top left shoulder of the initiate. Suddenly, so quickly that Kent could hardly follow its path, the blade scored a line across the man's bare chest and stomach, moving down in a diagonal until it reached the top of his right thigh.

The movement was repeated, beginning at the right shoulder and crossing downwards to the left thigh. At first, there was no discernable bleeding. The blade had cut so finely and cleanly that the skin had closed behind it. But now, as the choir sang with renewed strength and the initiate was annointed with perfumed oil on his head and shoulders, his body slowly blossomed into a bloody cross. He bled freely as he continued to stare dead ahead, unflinching throughout the ordeal. Obviously, this was desirable, for the next moment ripples of applause began to pass through the audience. It grew as the man was taken down and led away, his body a hideously streaked mask of blood. Kent began to feel nauseous, the room tipping before his eyes. Cold sweat broke on his forehead as he became aware that the best way of drawing attention to himself was by throwing up right now. He rose unsteadily to his feet, just as the others did, to applaud more loudly than ever. On the stage, another initiate was being led forward to the stand. All around him, men in the audience had torn open their shirts to reveal the criss-cross scars which signified their successful initiation into the society. Kent turned and stumbled away through the throng as fast as he could. He threw a backward glance at the stage as the speaker waited for the audience to resume their seats. He could no longer see Collis. Around him, the applause was dying down as people began seating themselves. Kent was aware that in a few seconds he would be the only one still standing. He looked wildly around. All the nearby seats were taken. He broke into a run. People began turning around to look at him. He had almost reached the door when a man rose from his chair and plucked at Kent's jacket. He pulled free and moved on. Another held out an arm.

'Where's your badge, fella?'

'Hey, buddy!'

'He's an outsider!' The call was quickly taken up. Someone stepped in front of the double doors ahead. The tall, anonymous figure stood with his arms outstretched. Kent balled his fist as he approached and punched the man as hard as he could in the stomach. The figure doubled in agony and keeled to one side. Kent pulled at the door handle. Behind him, several men were now moving towards the doors. Kent swung the door wide and left the hall at a run, pounding along the corridor as fast as he had ever moved in his life. Behind, the thick carpeting silenced the footfalls of his approaching pursuers. As he reached the elevator bank, he saw with amazement and thankfulness that one of the lifts was just departing the floor, and flung himself through the doors as they closed. Stabbing his floor button, he fell back against the wall trying to catch his breath while the men reached the outer doors below. High on the wall beside him, the handsome couple smiled serenely and successfully down from their cocktail bar stools. Kent retched.

Reaching his floor, he broke into a trot once more, pulling his pass card free from his back pocket as he did so. Behind him, he could hear another elevator arriving with a ping. He reached his room and thrust the crumpled card into the lock. The red light showed.

Oh God, pleaded Kent, please don't do this to me now!

He pulled the card free and flattened it out with his hand. In the distance he could hear the muffled, hurried approach of many people. He jammed the card into the lock once more.

Still red.

At the far end of the corridor, his pursuers appeared. He withdrew the card and pushed it back into the slot. Red. And again. They were twenty feet from him now. Red changed to green. Sobbing with relief, Kent turned the door handle and fell inside just as the first of the men reached him. In the darkness of the room he groped for the lock and safety chain, throwing them both on.

The searing pain in his chest began to subside as he caught his breath. Outside he could hear urgent whispered conversation. He knew they dared not make a noise at this time of night without disturbing guests in other rooms.

His forehead rested against the door as he breathed deep. He outstretched his arm and clicked on the light. Collis and two other men were seated before him, at the table and on the bed. Kent's stomach fell away.

'You English guys sure take fright easy,' said Collis as his partners rose and walked to the door. Collis shook his head sadly. 'You know, I really thought you'd make our first European convert after the way we talked the other night, but I guess you people aren't ready for it yet.' Kent heard the door being opened behind him. People swarmed in.

'What ... what's going to happen?' Kent's eyes were wide with fear.

'Oh, I guess we'll eventually make moves into the continent. Don't know if we'll bother with England, though. The rest of the world doesn't any more, you know. Quaint little place, but a waste of time commercially.'

'I meant about me ... about me!' said Kent, his voice rising.

'Oh, you. Well.' Collis looked to the others for confirmation. 'We have a standard procedure for dealing with this sort of situation.' Everyone nodded. Two of them seized his arms while a third began pulling at his shirt, ripping off the buttons. Collis smiled a big plastic smile.

'You get Cleansed. I mean, really Cleansed. It's the same as the other ceremony, only deeper. *Much* deeper.'

As the blade touched his bare shoulder his scream was cut off, too.

Citylink Nine

Norris was sitting on a low wall between two hedges cut neatly into globes. Untying his shoelaces, he wriggled his feet free and gently massaged them. After leaving the shuttered hotel, he had arrived at a subway station, and had succeeded in boarding what he took to be an Uptown train.

Sadly, it wasn't an Uptown train. It was an Under The River And Miles Away train, and discharged him in what appeared to be a vast suburban housing development. Since then he had not spotted a working telephone booth, a patrolman, a car or even another human being. He looked at his watch. Nearly 11.30 p.m. He gingerly slid his feet back into his shoes. For the past few minutes he had become resigned to the thought of flagging down a passing car, but since deciding on this plan there had been no more vehicles.

Perhaps he had died and gone to hell.

The travel bag had chafed a sore patch on his shoulder. He switched it to the other side and set out once more. On either side, topiarised hedges concealed low brick dwellings with darkened windows. The occupants of these suburban havens were presumably all in bed by now.

He reached a wide, deserted intersection and flipped a quarter to decide his next direction. Unfortunately, he threw it too high and failed to see where the coin fell. He had no more change. Norris bent double, resting his elbows on his knees. He was so incredibly tired. A bed, fresh linen, was that too much to ask? He felt like crying.

'Are you all right?'

Norris stood quickly and turned around. An attractive, smartly dressed woman of about forty-five stood watching him in puzzlement. She was swaying slightly. In one hand she held a lead, to which was attached a small hairy dog of indeterminate pedigree.

'Oh, no, I'm fine, thank you,' said Norris automatically, then realised that he wasn't any such thing.

'I thought you were throwing up.'

'No, I'm, er, well, actually I'm lost.'

'You're English, aren't you?'

Norris nodded.

'Do you have a cold?' She pointed to his layers of clothes, amusement playing in her eyes.

'Um, no.' By now, he was pretty tired of repeating the story. 'It's all rather complicated, but basically I need to find a hotel for the night.'

'My God,' laughed the woman, 'you're miles from the nearest one. Sparky, no!' She jerked the lead just in time to prevent the odd little dog from peeing on Norris's leg. 'If you like I can drive you to a hotel.'

'Oh, no,' Norris protested. 'I couldn't ask you to do that.' But he prayed she'd insist.

'I insist,' said the woman, holding out her free hand. 'My name's Gloria. Who the hell are you?'

'Norris, Andrew Norris,' said Norris, gratefully pumping her arm.

'I'll be happy to drive you, Andrew,' said Gloria.

'To be honest I'm so goddamn bored taking this dog out every night, the drive will cheer me up.'

Gloria's car was parked in the next road. When they reached it, she threw open the door of the Subaru and carelessly tossed the dog in. Norris was beginning to suspect, quite rightly as it turned out, that Gloria had been drinking. Heavily.

'When I was single,' said Gloria, starting the car and pulling out from the kerb with a force that threw Norris's head back against the seat rest, 'I used to live on the Upper West Side. God, I had so many friends! The parties, the nightlife! We actually used to sit around exchanging intelligent ideas, for Christ's sake.' She manoeuvred the car between two parked trucks at a speed Norris would not have attempted sober. 'Then I married Harvey and we moved here. You wanna know what depressing is? Having the head of your neighbourhood committee explaining lawn policy to you. Being fined for forgetting your pooper scooper. Hedge animals. Co-ordinated jogging teams. Now, that's depressing. Jesus, Andy, I'm dying in this environment!'

Sparky yelped as Gloria heaved the car around a sharp bend. The Subaru was straddling the line in the centre of the road, heading for who-knows-where.

'Harvey loves that dog,' she muttered, taking a swig from the silver flask she had pulled from the glove compartment. 'Let's see if I can find us a bridge on the way to your hotel and we'll throw the little fucker off it.' She wrenched the stick shift and the vehicle made a sudden leap forward.

Norris was beginning to fear for his life. He stared out of the window at the speeding streets and failed to find any clue that they were approaching town.

'Don't ever move to the suburbs, Mr Norris, not if

you value your sanity. We had a dinner party last night. Six of us spent four hours discussing drapes. The conversation was so sparse that at one point I thought I'd actually died.' She revved the engine. 'We're having pot roast tomorrow night, you should come over. Bring a book.'

Gloria suddenly swung the Subaru onto an iron-girdered bridge. As soon as she had righted the car, she reached over into the back seat. For a moment, Norris really thought that she was going to fling the dog out of the window, but she was just reaching for a cigarette.

'Take the wheel for a second, will you?'

'I, ah, don't drive …' Norris steered wide-eyed as Gloria rooted around in the rear, her ample bottom turned to him, her stiletto-shod feet barely touching the pedals. Weaving back and forth over the traffic lane, the car shot across the bridge and headed off into the night.

What Is Wrong With
This Picture?

The fire spans its flamelight over artificial coals while the television announcer gives details of the night's final programme: a talk show. Above the fireplace, a huge copper-finished eagle flies, a digital clock recessed in its tail feathers. The time is 11.36 p.m.

On the dining room table two plates still stand, scraped clean and ready to be taken to the kitchen. From the twenty-four-inch television set which dominates the corner of the dining room, the theme music of the talk show blares. Screams of laughter and hammering applause greet the host as he bounds down the stairs, pretending to be young and energetic. Beneath his tread, each step lights up. He shouts something at the audience, and they shout something back. He swings his fist to punctuate the double drumbeat which follows the greeting. He is very tanned, and wears a pale blue leisure suit.

Suddenly, the suit bleaches, the image flares and fades, the sound dies. The screen crackles into an electrical snowstorm.

On two comfortable modern seating units they rest before the sparkling, static-filled screen, still watching intently. After twenty years of marriage they have little to say to each other that will surprise or even interest, so they stay mostly silent. Their names are Ray and Mary Dixon. They have a grown-up daughter called Susan who lives on a neighbouring estate. I say 'estate', although the word is frowned upon by the property agents in the area. This smart collection of Crescents and Closes and Avenues is almost a town on its own, the main difference being that towns tend to have at least some kind of character.

Ray and Mary sit immobile, their eyes turned towards the shimmering brilliance in the corner of the room, and for a moment they too seem to shimmer. Ray's arms are folded. Mary's legs are crossed at the ankle. It is a cool, dry Thursday night in May, in a suburb of a suburb of Liverpool, in the North of England. But for the babble and squabble of the television, the house, and indeed the street, is peaceful.

Ray moves his arm to his side. Mary's legs uncross. In the dining room of No. 11, Ormiston Crescent, the Dixon family spend another quiet evening indoors, and there is something wrong with this picture.

Earlier on in the evening, everything had been normal enough. If we could stand on tiptoe and turn back the clock set in the tail of the copper-finished eagle, we would know.

It is now 6.29 p.m.

Mary clicked off the hoover with her foot and stood it upright against the skirting board. She pushed her peppery brown hair away from her eyes and walked to the window, letting a long breath escape from puffed red cheeks. Outside it was still light, the weak evening

170

sun refracting on the bonnets of the cars parked along the street. She turned to the clock. Ray would be home any minute now. Wiping her hands on her apron, she lifted the hoover and stowed it under the stairs, humming along with the inane, repetitive tune they had been playing all week on the radio. She checked herself irritably. She hated the song, but the local radio station was playing it so often that it had entered her subconscious, whether she liked it or not.

Mary heard the key turn in the front door lock, and peered around the corner. The door was a panel of frosted glass sailing boats, closing to reveal the heavy set figure of Ray, arriving home in an unfamiliar grey business suit. Since his heart attack, he had given up his job on-site at the local engineering works, and had taken a less physically demanding role in the company, offering advice from behind a desk. Mary had kept her morning job at a solicitor's office in Liverpool, and usually rode in with Ray, to return alone just after lunch with the shopping and the household chores before her. Tonight, she had prepared a casserole. She smiled at Ray, and asked him about his day. He in turn gave a pleasant, non-committal reply and headed for the bedroom to change out of his suit, just as he always did.

Over the evening meal, Mary watched Ray as he ate in silence. He had never really been handsome, and these days was running to fat. He was not a great conversationalist, and rarely took his wife out any more. He just wanted to live his life, and do so quietly, with the minimum of fuss and disturbance. Ray was fifty-five, and old before his time. But then, he always had been.

Sometimes, though, like now, as the evening sun-light faded through the window, and he thoughtfully ate with his knife and fork lowered by the sides of his plate, he looked to Mary like a small boy with the adventures of the world still before him. Ray's eyes came up from his meal and caught her gaze, holding and dismissing it wordlessly as he turned to the window.

When she was young, Mary had wanted to be an actress. More than anything, her dream had been to perform on the stage. But she had chosen her course too late, and had met Ray, and the dreams had changed to a course which led here, to Ormiston Crescent, to a detached new home like a thousand others, on an endless estate cut into a once green hillside.

In a way she liked it, because it simplified her life. The shops, the cinema, the local pub restaurant — these had become her stages. She organised work for charity, and outings for local groups, and told herself there was no time to be bored.

She used to wonder if there was something more. Now she knew that there wasn't.

Ray looked up and smiled absently, his plate clean. After the meal, Mary went into the kitchen to make tea while Ray settled down in front of the television. He started to watch a programme, then skimmed the headlines of the daily newspaper instead. The television featured a quiz show in which comedians he had never heard of impersonated other comedians he had never heard of. The newspaper told him what they all did when they weren't appearing on quiz shows. Together, the TV and the paper formed a hermetically self-serving circle. He rested his head back on a cushion and closed his eyes. Mary pottered on in the kitchen. Somewhere in the distance a dog was barking. Nothing happening here yet. Let's move the clock on.

8.17 p.m.

In the red and white kitchen, at the stainless steel sink, Mary rinsed a pastry dish and turned it over on the draining board.

'Ray?' she called out. 'Is there anything on TV? I'll come and sit down.'

No reply. She dried her hands on her apron and walked into the dining room, one half of which served as a lounge, and was decorated accordingly with hanging spider plants and china ornaments. Ray was slumped in the armchair, snoring lightly, his cushion on the floor. Mary removed the newspaper from beneath his arm and scanned the entertainment page for details of the evening's television programmes. She clicked the TV channels from 1 to 2 to 3, turning down the volume as she did so. Then she sat down in the orange corduroy seating unit near her husband, with the remote controlled channel selector in her lap, and continued to try different stations, frowning with annoyance as she did so. Sport. People shooting each other. Sport. People hitting each other. Switching back to the first channel, she found it had changed to show a stern-faced newscaster sitting behind a newsdesk. Mary looked up at the eagle-clock, puzzled. The news wasn't due until nine — another half-hour to go. She raised the sound slightly.

'And that is the end of the newsflash. We will interrupt our regular scheduled programmes with further news bulletins as soon as we have any more information.' The announcer's face turned into the face of a blonde American girl framed in pink satin sheets. Mary sighed and kicked off her slippers. She picked up the newspaper and began to read. In a few minutes, the words started to dance before her eyes and she fell into a gentle sleep.

173

She awoke with a sudden start at the noise, an enormous bang outside in the street. Ray sat up, startled and blinking. He looked across at Mary and climbed out of his armchair, crossed to the window and pulled back the curtain. Together they peered out into the dusky roadway beyond.

'Can't see anything ...'

'Ray, what was it?' Mary leaned forward and cupped her hand over the glass.

'Too loud to be a car backfiring. Nobody else is looking out of their windows. Funny.' Ray let the curtain fall back into place.

'Aren't Them Across The Street even having a look?'

'Couldn't see them. Couldn't see anyone.'

'Shouldn't you go outside and see what it was?'

'It wasn't anything. Just a noise, that's all. You go and sit down.'

Mary didn't answer. Her nerves were never very good at the best of times. Life varied little from day to day, and change of any kind disturbed her. Ray turned back to the televsion and switched channels. Mary returned to the window and looked out once more, then came and joined him. Together they watched ten minutes of a loud detective show. It was terrible, something about a Los Angeles policeman who could see through walls. Suddenly, the sound began to grow in volume until it distorted, and the picture started enlarging, bigger and bigger until they could see the coloured dots which made up the image on the screen.

There was a loud fizzing noise, and just as suddenly the detective show came back on. 'What on earth's wrong with this picture?' asked Ray, climbing out of the armchair and crossing around to the back of the TV set. He rolled up the sleeves of his shirt and began to play with the control knobs.

'Tell me when it's better.'

'It's already gone back to normal, Ray. Leave it alone.' Ray fiddled some more with the controls, then peered around to the front of the set.

'Is that better?'

'I told you, it's already gone back to normal.' Ray returned to his seat, irritated. They sat and watched some more of the detective show.

'You know the Bentall boy down the road? The one with the motorbike?' Mary had the exasperating habit of interrupting programmes whenever she started to lose interest in them.

'I'm watching this.'

'You said it was boring.'

'I know that, but ...'

'They caught him stealing. Not the first time, apparently ...'

'Well, what do you expect? There's nothing round here but cars and houses. I wonder what the kids are expected to do all day for excitement ...'

'They don't need excitement. Normal people don't ...' Mary ended in mid-sentence. The television screen showed a strange, expanding image again, the sound distorting and breaking up. Ray started out of his seat once more.

'I bet it's those bloody kids on the aerial.'

He left the room at a trot, while Mary stayed in her chair, worried.

She saw Ray pass in the hall.

'They'll have it down in a minute. I'll fix them.'

Ray closed the front door. Outside, here in the gathering dusk, the crescent was silent. Bonfire smoke rolled slowly over the back gardens of the detached houses sitting in the arc of the road. A soft pink mist lay over the woodland just beyond the gardens, and above it stretched a purple sky. There was a cool dampness in the air which had begun to condense into dew. Ray's shoes grew wet as he walked through the spring grass at the side of the house. He stepped away from the wall and looked upwards towards the roof. The television aerial stood glistening against the evening sky, untouched and unmoving. He turned his gaze across the road to the new houses opposite. In most of them, primrose squares of light showed from dinnertime lounge-diners. Few hallways or porches were yet lit. People only seemed to leave them on when they were going out. Along by the kerb stood a neat row of company cars, their engines ticking and cooling, their back windows condensing in the vaporous air.

Ray drew a deep breath. The bonfire smoke was sweet, and filled his lungs with a rich earthy scent. This was the only time of day when Ray felt close to the surrounding countryside, and not as if he was living on some vast paved building site. The estate stretched for miles in every direction, its curved white roads cutting through marsh and meadow alike. Each rise and combe was quaintly named, as if the originality of the street titles would make up for the suffocating blandness of the houses lining them. Ray returned indoors.

'It happened again while you were outside,' said Mary, more worried than ever. 'Suppose it blew up?'

'Don't be silly, Mary.' Ray scratched his bald spot and stared at the set. 'That's less than a year old. I'll give the rental people a call in the morning. Come and sit down.' Together they sat in the gathering darkness of the lounge. Outside, the streetlamps were coming on.

'I'm going to make some more tea,' said Mary, rising from her armchair. She felt vaguely unsettled,

176

sitting there with nothing to do. Sometimes, Ray would hire a videotape and they would play it on the machine Susan had bought them for Christmas, but the films weren't terribly good, and these days they bothered with it less and less. She had just finished knitting a shawl for Susan's new baby, and felt reluctant to start on another pattern immediately. She supposed she could sit and read a book ...

As she boiled the water for the tea, she looked across to the Fordes' house. Their kitchen light shone over the yard, filling the gap between the two houses. Occasionally the Fordes came over, bringing their horrible home-made wine with them, but their conversation seemed welded onto the familiar subjects of TV stars, tabloid press scandals and the welfare of various babies within the Forde empire. As she re-entered the lounge with the teatray, Ray looked up from the paper.

'I see that singer's got divorced,' he said, reading aloud.

'"'He beat me black and blue' sobbed the vivacious Sindy." Doesn't look very vivacious to me.'

The room fell silent. Ray finished his tea and sat back, watching the television with the sound turned off. This time the bang was so loud that it almost blew the windows in. Ray and Mary jump up as one.

'What the hell ...?'

'What on earth was that?' They crossed to the lounge window and looked out into the darkened street. There was nothing to be seen. The lights had gone out in the house opposite. Its windows stared darkly out to the neatly clipped front lawn.

'That was an explosion. I know that from the war.' Ray continued to stare out of the window, puzzled. Behind him, Mary wrung her hands in despair.

'What's happening, Ray?' she cried. 'I'm frightened. What is it?'

'Over the road. They might be hurt. Their lights are out. It might be the mains.'

'Don't go over there!' Mary grabbed his arm. Ray turned to her.

'I should go …' He looked back at the window.

'You will not! That's how people get killed. Call the police from here.'

Ray headed into the hall and picked up the telephone receiver. Moments later, Mary joined him. Ray dialled the operator.

'I'd like you to connect me to the police station. I'll wait.' He cupped his hand over the mouthpiece. 'Their lines are all busy.' The couple waited in silence.

'Hello? I'm sorry, you'll have to speak up, there's a lot of static on the line.'

Mary looked across to the television in the lounge. A newscaster was mouthing silently from behind his desk. Another newsflash. She ran over to the set and turned up the volume.

'Police are urging everyone to turn off their …'

'Mary, I can't hear what the police are saying. Turn that thing down.' She turned down the volume and crouched forward, trying to catch the announcer's words.

'Oh, it's no good. I can't hear. I'll try again in a few minutes.' Ray replaced the receiver. 'Why don't you go and do something in the kitchen? You know watching the news only makes you upset. Go on.'

Mary reluctantly left the television and gathered their teacups. She took them with her into the kitchen and stood them on the draining board. She turned on the hot tap and positioned the bowl beneath it. As the bowl filled, she stood staring blankly out of the window. She felt cold inside, vaguely disoriented, as if the familiar objects around her — the shelves and cupboards, the cutlery racks — were the trappings of someone else's home, someone other than her.

Just then something caught her attention. From the corner of her eye she saw — or seemed to see — a figure caught in the light at the front of the house next door.

There it was again — the figure of a young man dashing across the strip of drive between the two houses. Then the Fordes' kitchen light went out. The alleyway was thrown into darkness. Mary leaned forward, her face close to the window. She could hear movement outside. A crunch of gravel, then a faint cry. She backed away from the sink with her hand raised to her mouth.

'Ray,' she called hoarsely. 'Come here, quick!' She returned to the window and looked out. There, across the connecting alleyway, outlined in the jaundiced light of the sodium streetlamps, were the running figures of several people. Suddenly someone banged on the window and shouted something. Mary screamed and ran from the kitchen, pulling the door shut behind her. Ray came running up and put his arms around his wife.

'What's the matter? What is it?'

'A man. I think they're being burgled next door. I think someone ... someone's burgling the houses around us. The lights ... going out,' she said, very close to tears. Ray made to pull away, but Mary kept her grip.

'Don't! Don't go outside! Call the police again!' Mary held tight as her husband tried to pull toward the door.

'Look,' he began reasonably, 'there has to be a simple

179

explanation for this. This is an ordinary neighbourhood. Nothing odd happens in places like this. We're safe. I'm here with you.' Mary began to relax her grip a little. 'That's better. Calm down. Go and make some more tea.'

'I'm not going back in there,' said Mary, tensing again. 'Phone the police, please Ray. Please.'

'You're working yourself into a state, that's what you're doing.' Ray freed himself and went back to the telephone. He raised the receiver to his ear, then held it away, wincing at the high pitched screech emanating from it.

'Turn the sound up on the telly, and just sit down. I'll make the tea, and by that time the line should have cleared.' Ray turned and left Mary in the big armchair, staring at the TV screen as a black and white police car screamed around an L.A. street.

9.47 p.m.

'It was starlings.' Ray came bounding down the stairs. Mary looked at him, wringing her hands. 'That's what the noise was. Five or six of them.'

'How do you know?' Minutes ago there had been a series of thuds against the slope of the roof. Ray had gone to check.

'They're dead. They must have been flying at a fair lick. They fell into the garden.'

Behind them, the television speakers chattered and buzzed.

'It's going funny agin.' Mary looked back at the set and bit her bottom lip.

'Better turn it off. Might do permanent damage otherwise.'

'I'm sorry, Mary, but if the phone doesn't start working in the next few minutes. I'm going next door to use theirs.'

Ray headed into the kitchen and washed his hands at the sink. When he returned to the lounge-diner, he found his wife at the window pointing out.

'Look! Look! Oh, Ray!' The television screen showed lines of static. Ray joined Mary at the window. Five or six men were running helter-skelter down the street as if all the demons of hell were after them. In the distance there was another bang, and a flare of bright light. One of the young men slipped on the kerb and fell forward, tearing the skin from his face and hands. He stumbled to his feet, unaware of his bloody grazes, and began to run again.

Mary looked in the direction of the bang, and saw a light glowing more fiercely by the second. It seemed to be moving forward to the bend in the road. As it rounded the corner, they saw that it was a flaming car, rolling forward as jets of fire billowed from its windows. As it finally drew to a stop directly outside the Fordes' house, Mary whimpered and buried her head in Ray's shoulder, but he suddenly pulled free.

'I'm going outside to see what the bloody hell's happening,' he shouted.

'No!' screamed Mary, desperately hanging on to his arm. 'Ray! Whatever it is, it's dangerous. It's nothing to do with us! Please don't! Stay in!'

'I have to look. You stay here.' He made for the door.

The second he stepped outside he could feel the heat of the burning car against his face. In the distance there was shouting, faint and chaotic. He crossed the lawn to the Fordes' house and went up to the front door. There was a dead bird lying on the welcome mat before him. He kicked it aside and rang the bell. There was no response. He rang again, turning around to look at the car crackling and flaming in the gutter.

When he turned back he found himself staring through the fluted glass of the front door at Mr Forde, the moon-white face moving back and forth, mouthing something.

'Arnold!' called Ray. 'Open the door! What's happening here?' Forde's voice was muffled, but he understood the message clearly. The mouth was saying 'Go away! Go away!' again and again. The hands rose and made violent shooing gestures. Ray stood back from the door, astounded.

Inside, Mary could see Ray from the window. Suddenly the television static ceased and she heard an American voice.

'When did you find the body, Smokey?' She turned to see the ciphers on the now clear screen, familiar people in familiar roles — tough as nails police chief, no-good small time crook — each actor more cosy and familiar than her own next door neighbours. She turned from the television back to the window, and began to cry.

The crackling wreck of the car belonged on the screen, not out there on the street. She had to treat what was happening outside as if it were a TV programme, safe behind glass. All she could do — all she could ever do — was watch.

Ray stood in the street watching the dying flames of the car. Across the street he saw another white face at the window, watching from the darkened room. And at the window of his own house stood Mary, shocked and tearful. He had no idea where the nearest phone-box was. He checked his trouser pockets for his car keys, found them and headed for the garage.

In the darkness of the side alley he approached the green double doors with a growing sensation of panic.

He produced the correct key and twisted it in the lock. Another bird stumbled feebly at his feet. He kicked at it hard, revolted, and pulled at the garage door. They seemed to come from nowhere, a man and a woman, falling from the black corner of the alley.

'Help us! Get inside! You must help us!' The woman grabbed Ray's arm and the keys went spinning into the dark. The man stumbled and fell heavily against him.

'Let us in! You have to let us in!' Ray could feel the woman's hot, feverish breath on his neck. He tried to turn and pull free, but the woman hung on.

Inside, Mary saw Ray leave the front door of the Fordes' house and stand before the burning car. Then he was off, striding up the driveway toward the garage. She knew then that he was going for the car, but before she could decide what to do, the voice of the television cut into her thoughts. She turned and saw the newsflash announcer as Ray came crashing in through the back door, throwing the bolts across as soon as he had done so. She was aware of him entering the room, aware of the shouts and banging at the rear of the house, but most conscious of the newsreader's public school voice. Empty and drained, she fell onto the orange seating unit beside the television.

'Further information just in,' said the stately, disembodied voice. 'An electrical malfunction has been blamed for the massive bacterial spill at the Courtwell Testing Plant earlier this evening, when an electronically operated processor released a drum of toxic germicidal gas into the atmosphere. Following reports of panic in the South Liverpool area earlier tonight, police are advising families on the estates bordering Courtwell to stay indoors and switch off all electrical appliances until further notice.

'Courtwell officials stress that the chemical, if

ingested, will cause massive neurological imbalance and fever symptoms, followed by disruption and deterioration of the skin tissue. People are urged once again to stay in their houses until the extent of the damage can be estimated. All appliances ... '

11.37 p.m.

The talk show host holds up his hands to stem the applause and laughter. He turns once more to his guest.

'But seriously, now, Sindy,' he says, grinning to the audience. 'What is your advice to the man who tries to pick you up?'

The vivacious Sindy seems about to reply. Her lovely lips part in answer, and her face distorts, the eyes twisting around, the skin between them stretching apart as the screen dissolves once more into a welter of static.

The numerals tick over in the tail of the copper-finished eagle, and the grease slowly hardens on the dinner plates. Ray and Mary sit before the glittering screen, for all the world as if they are spending another quiet evening in front of the television.

Mary yawns. Beneath her opalescent skin a million bacterial microbes burrow and spiral, twisting and turning, their sheer weight and number forcing her skin to pulse and pucker. Ray's arms unfold as a billion identical germcells attack and invade and devour, moving in every direction at once, stretching and convulsing his body. Ray's arm hits the remote control selector and the static vanishes from the screen for once and for all.

In the new silence of the lounge, Ray and Mary sit side by side, the thin skin of their sac-like bodies shimmering as it fights to contain a new, less easily contented form of life.

184

Citylink Ten

They had travelled the length of FDR Drive in record time, largely due to the fact that Gloria was completely ignoring the speed limit.

'What's that noise?' asked Norris with a sudden start.

'What noise?' said Gloria, who was now the right way up in the driver's seat, but still keeping the speedo at sixty. The interior of the car was suddenly filled with pulsing red light.

'Oh my God, it's a police car,' cried Norris. 'Slow down!'

'Are you kidding? Do you have *any idea* how drunk I am? You think I normally drive like this?' She put her foot to the floor and the Subaru shot ahead. 'We can outrun 'em in this baby, no problem.' She swung the wheel hard to the right and the car sped onto South Street in a headlong rush toward Battery Park. Gloria revved the engine hard. Behind them, Sparky did an involuntary somersault. The river, its oily surface glittering in the moonlight, flashed by between darkened buildings. In the distance, the flashing red lights reappeared, accompanied by a high-pitched whoop. Norris grabbed at Gloria's arm in desperation.

'Gloria, it's not worth it! They're going to catch up

with us. Please!' The car mounted a low kerb and caught the corner of a bale of leaflets, bursting them across the hood and fountaining hundreds of sheets into the sky. Several stuck themselves across the windscreen. Gloria peered over the wheel and found herself staring at the words JESUS IS ALWAYS WITH YOU. 'He better be driving something with decent acceleration,' she said. More leaflets fell across the windscreen.

'Andy,' she shouted. 'I can't see a Goddamn thing! Can't you climb out on the hood and do something?'

The car overshot a bend in the road. Two wheels hammered up onto the deserted sidewalk. The police car added a burst of speed and almost rear-ended them.

'Driver in the Subaru, pull over!' boomed an amplified voice.

'Oh God, please do as they say!' shouted Norris. He leaned out of the passenger window and looked back at the squad car. 'I'm being abducted by a madwoman!' Gloria grabbed his shirt and pulled him back in. 'You don't seem to understand,' he shouted at her, 'we'll both be thrown in jail!'

'You think I'm not in jail now?' she asked, her face crumpling as she started to sob.

'Give me the wheel!' Norris fought for control, but Gloria pushed his hands away and stamped hard on the gas pedal. There was a thud on the back of Norris's seat as Sparky performed another aerial stunt, and the Subaru overshot the approaching curve by about a hundred and twenty feet.

For a moment it seemed that the car had sprouted wings and would fly gracefully over the river, touching down gently on the other side. Seconds later it slammed down as if plunging from a Coney Island waterchute. From inside the vehicle came two cries of 'Shiiiiiiiiit!' and the unusual sound of a dog screaming.

Loaded Blanks

The sudden rainstorm had brought the homegoing traffic to a standstill. Morrisey sat behind the wheel and fumed. Five lines of cars were attempting to filter into four traffic lanes, vehicles inching forward as much as they dared, fighting for every square foot of tarmac. The crimson brake lights of the Audi in front turned the rain spattering the windscreen into droplets of blood. Morrisey toyed with the radio, trying to find some news of the traffic flow ahead, then angrily snapped it off. His thirty-minute journey home had already taken him forty-five minutes, and he was still little more than halfway there. Sanya would no doubt be furious, as he had promised to leave the office early tonight, and instead had left even later than usual thanks to a stack of medical reports which the computer had for some reason seen fit to file by insurance profile instead of age.

The car behind blared its horn long and loud, but none of the drivers around it paid any attention. There was nowhere Morrisey could move to. His little Volkswagen was already stuck diagonally between two lanes in an attempt to squeeze into the correct traffic stream. He turned and gave an exaggerated shrug to the impatient driver behind, while the rain thrummed on the roof above with renewed vigour.

The lights changed and the traffic crept forward. In front of the Audi, an old blue Ford Cortina picked this moment to stall. Morrisey watched in fascination as the driver in front raged and swore, thumping his car horn with the heel of his hand. The Ford started up again, jerked forward a few feet and stopped so suddenly that the Audi behind bumped it. Morrisey applied his brake and looked in his rear view mirror. Behind him, an elderly lady was clambering between the boxed-in vehicles with her shopping bags held high in a desperate attempt to get across the road. He turned his attention back to the scene through the windscreen. The driver of the Audi had now jumped out of his car, and was storming up to the Ford. A smart young executive type, the man had even in his rage closed his own car door so that the rain would not damage the interior upholstery. Now he was banging on the side window of the Ford as its elderly driver looked up in astonishment.

The ability of people to work themselves up into a state over a minor mishap rarely surprised Morrisey. As a doctor and one-time sociology lecturer, he had a tendency to regard himself as somewhat of a dispassionate observer of the human race.

Through the racing rain on the glass, Morrisey watched the executive haranguing the Ford driver to little effect. The traffic lights were changing again, but vehicles at the crossroads had solidly blocked the path ahead. On either side of him, people sat patiently behind their wheels waiting for the road to clear. Many stared blankly ahead, their fingers tapping the dashboard in time with the radio jingles.

Morrisey's attention was pulled back to the scene

before him by the sudden sound of shattering glass. The executive had punched through the side window of the Ford, and with a bloody fist was attempting to grab the neck of the terrified old man, who was pulling away, trapped in his seat by the tightly strapped seat belt. Suddenly, the executive seemed to slump, his sodden shoulders falling as he withdrew his bleeding arm from the smashed window. He slowly turned his head to the sky and screamed, his mouth a dark broad circle. Nobody moved from their vehicles, including Morrisey, who sat staring at the man in horror. On reflection, he realised that he should have done something at this point. But now the man had stopped screaming, and had dropped his head on his chest, as if suddenly unplugged from his source of energy.

Mechanically, he reached forward to the shattered window of the Ford and thrust his head inside as the terrified driver backed away. Morrisey was fighting with his seat belt when the young man lowered his face onto the edge of the glass. He was half out of the car when the long white throat was pressed to the jagged edge and pulled sideways along, and he was running across the rain-slick tarmac as the man fell back against the side of the Ford watching his blood pumping gently and persistently from his torn throat into the breast of the sopping suit jacket and onto the roadway at his feet.

Morrisey tried to staunch the flow of blood as he knelt on the road amidst the gathering crowd, but the jugular was ripped in several places, and the young man's body was fast emptying. He held the twitching torso flat, removing and balling his tie, and forcing it into the young man's mouth as he bit and snapped, but the body was still and cooling before the ambulance could pass through the surrounding traffic.

Morrisey gave his report to the police, refusing their offer of a ride home, but pulled his own car over when his hands started shaking so violently that he could no longer hold the wheel.

Sanya tried to understand. Of course she knew that Morrisey had had to stay and report. There was nothing else he could have done for the lad. But she failed to comprehend why no one else had come forward to help.

'Why did no one offer? Why should you be the one to go to the inquest and get involved?' Sanya tossed back hair of glossy jet and sighed. She crossed the scruffy, cluttered lounge and sat on Morrisey's knee with her arms around his neck. She was tiny, and as light as a feather.

'In my country, life is much more a matter for fate,' she said, her face close to his. 'We leave a man to follow his own path, and if he chooses to die, it is his right. Western people always think they must change this. Oh Sammy ...' She hugged him tightly as Morrisey pressed into the warmth of her body and asked himself why on earth anyone should have done such a terrible thing.

Margaret was sitting on the edge of his desk peeling an apple with a Swiss army knife. For a forty-six-year-old woman, she often looked like a little girl. Her ingenuous movements always surprised Morrisey. He leaned forward in his typing chair and dangled a typewritten page before her.

'I'm sure she thinks I should have just left him there to die,' he said.

'Sam, he *did* die. And it doesn't sound like you could have done much to prevent him from dying.'

'Now you sound like Sanya,' said Morrisey, irritably. 'There are very few western practices she approves of, what with her self-healing and her acupressure, and her leave-it-all-to-fate to sort out. What she sees in me I don't know.'

Margaret finished peeling the apple and dropped the single unbroken strand of peel into Morrisey's waste bin. She carefully folded the blade of the knife in and pocketed it within the voluminous folds of her skirt.

'Oh, you have a certain tarnished appeal,' she said, holding out her hand. 'What's this?'

Morrisey passed the piece of paper to her. 'The man who went berserk. I thought that perhaps he was an epileptic, but there's no record of that. It's from the coroner's report. An ex-colleague of mine.'

'Let's see, name of Dennis Haun. Twenty-nine. Married, two kids. No history of psychiatric problems. Estate agent — well, I suppose that could be classed as a high-pressure job.' Margaret flicked a cigarette from her pack and lit it thoughtfully.

'You shouldn't smoke so much.'

'It's this or another apple. Leave me alone. Never even been hospitalised. Seems normal enough.'

'Normal enough to cut his throat in the middle of a traffic hold-up,' said Morrisey.

'Sam, tell me you're not this naïve.' Margaret looked at him over the top of her bifocals. She had been acting head of the psychiatric unit at the institute for the past three years now, and when they had first met, Morrisey had been so shocked by the woman's forthright, almost offensive honesty that he had never suspected they would become firm friends within that first year.

More recently, they had entered into a vaguely

flirtatious working relationship which allowed them both to give vent to their anger and frustration at the antiquated working structure of the institute by getting good and drunk together a couple of times a month. Morrisey's hand scrubbed through his beard. He felt overworked and dead-ended in a world of academic theory and paperwork, but hardly naïve.

'This sort of thing happens almost daily in the big cities,' Margaret was saying. 'What do you expect? We pen people up in apartment blocks, pin down their leisure hours, point to a big billboard in the sky with a picture of beautiful people on it and say to them: That's how you should be. Laughing, tanned, rich and forever young. Now go and achieve it.' She blasted the ceiling tiles with a column of cigarette smoke. 'Then we all act surprised when they fall short of the mark and break down. Everyone was horrified when they discovered serial murderers, remember?'

Morrisey recalled one such recent tabloid sensation uncovering a murderer who had been killing at random over several years.

'Maybe they've always been around,' he said. 'Could be just that the papers weren't gunning for a new name and angle back then.'

'Maybe,' Margaret conceded. 'But you must admit that what we're seeing the emergence of in the latter part of the twentieth century is a new kind of motive-less violence which we haven't found a way to prevent building up.' She punctuated her nervous, rapid-fire speech with drags on her stubby cigarette. 'The yanks think they have the system licked. They groom their people beautifully. The kids are aimed at success from the start. Win at football, be a cheerleader, appear in the high school yearbook — "Most Likely To Succeed", successful career, straight teeth, perfect bodies prised into designer jeans. If your marriage screws up, analysis will repair the damage. If the cracks appear, paint right over them because you must never look weak.' She stubbed out the cigarette and flicked it into the bin. 'There's no big difference between America and China. Bad news is covered up.'

'Phew.' There was a pause. 'And I always thought you wanted to live in America.'

'Me? Good God, no. It's too bright over there. Too sunny and sporty and confident. There are no warm, dark hiding places for us insecurables to curl up in. I want you to take a look at something.'

Margaret rose and crossed to a battered grey filing cabinet, and withdrew a dogeared cardboard folder.

'This is my special file,' she said with a grin, handing it to Morrisey.

Inside were wads of typed pages, printouts and newspaper clippings.

'Suicides.'

Morrisey held up a computer readout filled with statistics.

'The figures are much lower for women, aren't they?' he asked.

'Oh, yes. 107 per million in males, just 65 per million in females. That was in, let me see a second ...' Margaret leaned across Morrisey, bringing with her a plume of smoke from a freshly lit cigarette. '1979.'

'And what's the figure now? Up or down on that?'

'Well, '83 is the last available year I have statistics for, and that was, um, 116 per million males and 58 per million females.'

'Males rising, females falling? I wonder why.'

'There's been some fluctuation in the population make-up, but even so, one of the problems facing us is that formerly stable statistics are no longer reliable.

Figures for acts of violence are going haywire. The old patterns just don't hang true anymore. There are a lot more disturbed people walking the streets, Sam.' Margaret crossed to the window and stared out as Morrisey leafed through the file.

'How long have you been collecting these things?'

'Just a couple of months. Amazing what happens in such a short time.'

The file before Morrisey contained details of hundreds of random acts of violence, from cases of murder and suicide, to the kind of absurd occurrences which filled the 'People Are Crazy' columns in magazines. Margaret turned from the window.

'I have a friend, an ex-patient, who's a stringer for a couple of the nationals. He started noticing a weird new statistic in city violence — the rise of the pointless crime. He sends me clippings like this.' She reached across him and turned to a page at the back of the file, pointing out a newspaper article about a teenage boy who had been found dead in an open-air swimming pool.

'He died of exposure. Couldn't leave the pool because his wrists and ankles had been tied together with barbed wire. They caught the couple responsible. Man and a woman from somewhere up North. They admitted that they'd beaten him unconscious with a piece of gas barrel, then tied him up and thrown him in the pool. The odd part is, they can't remember why on earth they did it. They didn't know the kid. Just drove around town looking for someone, and he happened to be in the right place at the wrong time.' Margaret leaned forward, wreathed in smoke. 'The couple weren't even interested in their own trial verdict. A textbook case, as these things go.'

'And you're making a hobby of collecting these

things?' Morrisey shuffled the clippings with a look of distaste, but his eyes were bright with interest.

'Not a hobby. I'd like to draw a few red lines on a graph. See what's happening in this fair town.' She looked at Morrisey and cocked an eyebrow.

'You're asking me to endorse this as a special project,' Morrisey said, waving the folder at her.

'Oh, come on Sam, you're as interested in this as I am, and you know it. Let's find out *why* an ordinary man kills himself in a traffic jam. Or this ...' She pulled open the folder once more and found a clipping. 'MAN IN ROOFTOP DEATH PLUNGE!' screamed the headline. '"He was one of the happiest, most contented men in the world,' said his wife, blonde ..." etcetera, etcetera ...' Margaret looked up in disgust. 'God knows why they have to report her hair colouring. But you can see we've got more than enough to start statistical analysis on.'

'All right,' said Morrisey. 'I'll put it up to the group.'

'No, Sam!' Margaret was indignant. 'This is my idea. Just give me a few hours down time on the computer this week, and I'll share the glory with you.'

After a minute's thought, Morrisey gave in with grace.

On the first Monday of the following month, Morrisey travelled up to Manchester to deliver a lecture. He returned home late the same night to find Sanya sitting at the kitchen table in tears. Without having to ask, he knew what the cause of the trouble was. He threw his briefcase down into a corner and drew her up into his arms.

'She hates me so much, Sam. I never took you away,' she sobbed as he cradled her head with his large hands. 'She had already left you. Always she phones to say hateful things.'

Joan, Morrisey's ex-wife, had lately taken to the bottle, and a wheedling campaign of harassment, mostly aimed at his new girlfriend. Sanya pushed away his hands and brushed the shining hair from her eyes.

'She won't divorce you ever, Sam. Is too big a mistake to admit.'

'Don't say that, Sanya. You know how much I love you. Just be patient.' He knew instantly that he had said the wrong thing. Sanya was the most patient woman he had ever met. He also knew that she was waiting for him to make some kind of move which would force a change in the situation.

'If you just let me get through this term, I'll sort the situation out. Please, Sanya. As soon as I've cleared my workload we'll go away somewhere. Somewhere peaceful.'

But now he was talking to a retreating figure, heading for the bathroom. The door closed quietly and firmly, leaving Morrisey standing in the centre of the shabby little lounge in exhausted confusion.

He turned on the television. Two beautiful, tanned people smiled at the camera as they sipped soft drinks by the side of a sun-fractured pool.

He felt like kicking in the screen, but poured himself a large scotch instead.

'Here's a good one. Self-immolation. The guy poured petrol over himself in the middle of a field. No reason given. A picture, look.'

Margaret held up a newspaper photograph showing a pile of charred remains.

'Please, I'm eating.'

'You should take a proper lunch, instead of that fried

chicken crap,' she said, slowly peeling her third apple of the day. 'Nothing new on the traffic jam man, then.'

'Dennis Haun? No.' Morrisey looked into the box of chicken and back at the newspaper photograph. He swallowed and closed the box lid.

'I wonder if he knew.'

'Knew what?'

'Why he was doing it. I wonder if he died still not knowing or understanding his actions.'

'Perhaps things just got too much for him and he snapped. Happens to me all the time.'

'OK, but if you've had a rotten day at the office, you don't go out and kick in a bus shelter, or drink bleach, or set fire to yourself. Want some apple?' Margaret offered him a slice on the blade of her knife. She had managed to remove the peel in one piece, as always.

'I *hate* apples. You only eat them to release nervous tension.'

'Wrong. To relieve tension I eat an entire cheese-cake. Let's get out of here, it's nearly nine thirty.' Margaret stood and brushed down her sweater. Her hair was tied back neatly in a ponytail, only her eyes showing the strain of the day.

'How's Sanya?'

'Bad. Joan's been calling and taunting her about the divorce, or lack of. She's getting very jittery about me working late.'

'Like tonight.'

'Like tonight,' agreed Morrisey, turning out the light and closing the door behind them. As they walked across the forecourt, heading for the carpark, Margaret turned and looked up at the moon, as it appeared and vanished behind fast-moving clouds.

'Perhaps that's the cause of the trouble.' She pointed upward.

'And you, a woman of science!' snorted Morrisey. 'That's all I need, for you to turn Druid on me. Still,' he considered, 'why not, eh? Everything else in my life is going crazy.'

As he fumbled with his keys, trying to open the door of the car, Margaret noticed that his hands were shaking.

She stared after Morrisey as he impatiently swung his car out of the driveway.

When he arrived back at his crumbling Victorian apartment, he found Sanya sitting in front of the TV watching the upmarket soap adventures of an oil-rich Texan family.

'You never watch this,' he said, following her eyeline to the screen. 'I thought you hated things which weren't realistic. I mean, look at the way they dress, for God's sake.' He threw down his coat and went to the bedroom. Sanya ignored him, and continued to stare at the screen. He stuck his head around the door.

'Sanya? You all right?' He ran a tired hand over his face and sighed. 'Do you want to go out to dinner tonight?'

'No, Sam. I don't want anything. Just leave me alone and I'll be fine.'

He could see that she was far from fine right now, but was too tired to think of a way of improving the situation. It was a safe bet that Joan had called again tonight. At Christmas she had agreed to a divorce, but as the date of the court proceedings grew nearer, it seemed her rationality was receding as her alcohol dependence increased. The legal web was growing larger daily, and Morrisey found the endless phone-calls taking up more and more of his working hours.

So it was not until after two weeks of domestic arguments and missed appointments that Morrisey knocked on Margaret's office door.

'I've brought you something for all the cancellations,' he said, producing a rather limp cluster of primroses. Margaret took the cigarette from her mouth and eyed them suspiciously. 'You took these from the windowbox next door.'

'It's the thought that counts. How's our little project coming along?'

Margaret's brow furrowed as she crossed to the filing canbinet and produced four huge folders stuffed with pieces of paper.

'Not so little, I'm afraid.' She dumped the files onto her desk. 'There are literally thousands of cases coming in which simply fail to fall into any category at all. From the local press, mostly, articles usually tucked away at the back of the paper. You don't get a good story out of something with no explanation, and that's what these clippings all have in common. They're all acts of violence with no justification. But the computer's come up with a couple of sets of figures.' She produced about five yards of computer paper covered in numerals.

'Christ,' said Morrisey. 'When you take up a pet cause there's no stopping you.'

'This is no "pet cause", Sam,' she said. 'There's something very peculiar happening. Look. We categorised these cases, all of which occurred between March 26th last year and February 15th this year. Each category was logged by type of crime, sex and age of instigator. There are over thirty headings, including self-inflicted wounds, destruction to property, murder, suicide, child abuse, sexually related crimes, non-chargeable arrests and so on.

'I then got the computer to check acts of violence with phases of the moon. No real correlation there. So I tried family background. But these cases are spread right through every social stratum. I also drew a blank with histories of mental illness. We have no real details in many of the cases, which doesn't help. Now ...' Margaret ran her hand over perforated sheets of numbers in an effort to locate further information. Graph lines ran from each category across several sheets. Each line was split in two, to denote males and females.

'The lines represent the incidence of violent acts over this given period,' said Margaret, nervously pulling on her cigarette. Morrisey followed the chart across with his finger, then sat back, amazed.

'You're telling me this is accurate?'

'See for yourself.'

'What I see is a median line rising almost vertically, and nearly doubling its rate of increase every three to four months.'

'Funny, that's what I see, too. And guess what, I had some first-hand experience yesterday. Woman on the bus just started screaming her head off. They had to pull her off the bus. I got up and ran after her, asked her what was the matter. She smiled and told me that she didn't have the faintest idea.'

'She might just have been a loony, you know,' said Morrisey, smiling.

'No, Sam. I mean, she was wearing expensive perfume. Dressed for a career job. Loonies don't doll themselves up before coming out and going crazy on the streets.'

'Well, I don't see why not,' Morrisey sighed, running his fingers through his thinning hair. He looked at the papers spread out before him once more. 'It seems like we have an epidemic on our hands.'

'But an epidemic of what?'

Morrisey only wished he knew.

'This is ridiculous. I won't have you do it.'

'You have no choice in this matter, Sam,' said Sanya. 'I have to go now. We discuss the whole thing later, yes?'

'No!' he shouted. 'We discuss it right now,' but he knew that this was not the right time. The day had been long and disastrous, the evening journey home was hell, and he had arrived to find Sanya waiting for him in the lounge with her suitcases around her.

'Don't shout at me, you never shout at me before,' she said softly, looking up at him.

'I'm sorry, Sanya. Please, just stay tonight and we'll talk it all through in the morning.'

'You have to be at office by seven thirty in the morning, Sam. They called for you, urgent. We will not talk.'

'All right,' said Sam, trying to find a way to reason, 'but if all this is about the divorce, then I can work it out. I've spoken to Joan …'

'And so have I.' Sanya stood and picked up her bags. The size of them made her seem even tinier than usual. 'Is just everything, Sam, not just divorce. We both come home each night too tired to even try with each other. What is point of living like this? You to go work, you stay late. Come in tired. We eat junk, live like robots. I have to go home.'

'Sanya,' he pleaded. 'I need you, please … it's too late for you to go home tonight.'

'No, I go to my real home. Back with my family. Tonight I stay with a girlfriend near the airport. I have left a letter.'

She smiled sadly at the door. 'You had to make a choice, Sam, and this you could not do. I have now to make this choice for you. You are a very good man, but we are not good together. You will find someone for you.' Sanya left, closing the door gently behind her.

An hour after, Morrisey was physically sick. He did not sleep that night, or the next.

'Shut up a minute. So this guy wins the pools, OK?' Margaret sat on the edge of her desk reading from a large red folder which she supported with one hand. In the other she waved a cigarette. Behind her, the files and newspaper clippings had grown into tottering stacks. Morrisey sat in front, listening.

'He has everything to live for. Three days after receiving the cheque he gets up early, tiptoes down to the garage in his pyjamas, and tries to burn off his face with a blowlamp. When they got to him ...'

'I haven't had lunch yet, if you don't mind,' said Morrisey, gingerly touching his stomach. Margaret looked at his uncombed hair, and the rings beneath his eyes.

'Are you getting any sleep at all these days?' She laid a hand on his shoulder. 'You know, I think it would help if you accepted the fact that she isn't coming back.'

'Thank you, doctor,' said Morrisey sarcastically. 'You know my reports must be in by Friday. Do you want me to make any mention of this?' He waved his hand across the computer readouts on Margaret's desk.

'I don't think we're ready for presentation yet,' she said cautiously. 'I have a theory of my own, to do with our old friend the Break-Even point. Give me a cigarette and I'll explain.' She accepted the cigarette and lit it, pulling the smoke down deeply and blowing it at the ceiling with obvious satisfaction. Around her, afternoon sunlight filtered weakly into the green-painted government office.

'If you remember, the Break-Even is a balancing point between what we want from our lives and what we see others getting. TV programmes and newspaper articles dwell on the lives of the successful. They capture the public imagination. But the public really want the successful to fail. All those "Success wrecked by drug addiction" stories are a smash with the public, because in our eyes the successful have too much and deserve to suffer. So we strike a balance — what we want, what we get. And if we see ourselves straying too far from the balance, we get angry. What's happening out there,' she gestured behind herself to the window, now lightly spattered with rain, 'is that the slightest extra pressure seems to be upsetting the balance.'

'Why?'

'Pressures of work,' shrugged Margaret. 'City living, who knows? It's a cumulative thing, and now it's a feeling that's affecting more and more people.'

'Wait, you're saying that this, this disease is limited to city dwellers?'

'Very much so. And it's especially amongst people in the new conurbations, those glamorous looking concrete wastelands they advertise on TV.'

'So what can be done?'

'I suppose, ultimately, we have to find a way to channel those feelings off …' said Margaret, watching Morrisey as his hands nervously tied and untied themselves.

The desk lamp still threw a cone of warm light into the centre of the darkened study. Morrisey sat staring at the papers before him, his eyelids already beginning to feel heavy again. He looked at his watch and was surprised to find it past midnight.

Dennis Haun.

Twenty-nine years old.

Wife. Two kids. Promotion in view. New house. New car. Hobbies: golf, swimming, cinema.

Margaret was wrong. There was no lack of balance in Haun's life. He was as successful as any of the smiling models on the billboards. He had more than most, materially speaking. Maybe he just hated traffic jams. Maybe something just snapped. Morrisey stood and stretched his back. Then he turned off the desk light and made his way to an empty, unmade bed.

'What are you taking for it?'

'For what, for Chrissake?'

'Well, you're obviously not sleeping. I suspect you're taking amphetamines to help get you through your reports, you nearly bite my head off every time I speak to you, so I guess you could call it depression.' Margaret looked very professional this morning in a smart grey business suit, legs crossed at the ankle, taking notes on her lap. Morrisey felt like one of her patients. He wondered if there was a couch he could lie on.

'Margaret, put yourself in my position,' he pleaded. 'The reports are needed for the international conference, and that begins next Tuesday. I've nowhere near completed them as it stands ...'

'... And you're going home to an empty flat ...' said Margaret, annoyingly.

'That's got nothing to do with it.'

'How are you spending your spare time?' she asked, lighting up as she did so.

'*What* spare time? What do you want from me, card tricks?' Morrisey slammed the back of the chair with his fist. 'I spend every spare minute worrying what's going to happen next.'

Margaret looked Sam coolly up and down. Uncleaned shoes, dishevelled suit, beard growth. Two days earlier, she'd had a disturbing conversation with Sam's immediate superior. Since Sanya had left, about a month ago, Sam's work had taken an erratic turn. He had given a bizarre, almost nonsensical lecture at Middlesex Polytechnic. He seemed forgetful. He was certainly drinking heavily. Could she see him on a strictly non-professional basis, purely to discover if he was happy working at the institute? She could.

But she was finding nothing out.

'What about sex?'

'I have no interest and no energy …'

'Has Sanya been in touch with you?'

'She called by to pick up the rest of her things. I helped her pack.'

'And since then?'

'She's back home now. She'll write, she won't call. Just in case I start on her.'

'Start on her?'

'Lose my temper.'

She made a note. She had never known Sam lose his temper over anything.

'Any how do you feel about that?' she asked, writing.

'Stop sounding like a fucking psychiatrist. I'll see you around.' Morrisey rose and collected his jacket. 'Next you'll be asking me if I hated my father.' He turned on her. 'I don't need this from you. You're supposed to be my friend, not some bloody government spy.' She could see that his hands were shaking violently as he reached for a cigarette.

'What do you mean by that?'

'Oh, come on. Don't tell me you weren't asked to give me the once over.'

Margaret lowered her notebook and looked thoughtfully over her glasses.

'Yes they have asked me. But I would have done anyway.'

'I bet you would have.' Morrisey moved toward her, his face colouring. 'You're so bloody smug, you and your theories. You know why I don't want you to submit your project?'

Margaret shook her head. She had never seen him this way, angry and irrational.

'Because you're wrong!' he shouted at her. 'People aren't screwing up because of the pressure. If life was simple when they were kids, and it's not now, well tough shit, because it's the same for all of us. Life gets more complex the older you get. Bills, telephones, bleepers, cars, arrangements, meetings, crowding you out of your life. You want to know why your computer can't work out what's happening? Because it doesn't understand the way people really think. It can't see that the busier life gets for us all, the emptier it is.'

With one swipe of his hand he cleared the stack of folders from the desktop and watched as they cascaded against the far wall.

'You want to channel that anger into something useful? Throw a little more light on human behaviour?'

He advanced on her. 'That's funny, Margaret, I thought you liked being in the dark. Isn't that what you said?'

'Sammy ...' Margaret started up from her seat, but Morrisey shoved past her and out into the corridor.

Outside, the rain thundered onto the rooftops of the cars in the institute forecourt. Morrisey slammed the door of the Volkswagen and started up the engine. Grinding gears, he pulled out of the drive and cut across the traffic lanes ahead. Behind him, Margaret ran to her car and jumped in.

Further up ahead, in the teeming evening traffic, she could just make out the roof of the VW. She was terrified that in his rage, he might do something stupid. The rain, the cars, the memory of Dennis Haun — it was too dangerous for her to let him out of her sight.

Two cars ahead, the lights suddenly changed and Morrisey's Volkswagen managed to slip through. Margaret watched the traffic slow to a stop all around her, and swore aloud. Across the junction, the VW was retreating behind a veil of rain and darkness. She stared blankly at the litterstrewn dashboard before her, at the empty cigarette packs and the dried apple peelings, at the old newspapers and the McDonald's boxes. The lights were still red. Perhaps they were stuck.

She picked up the curling, unbroken peel from the dashboard and ran it between her fingers, staring blankly through the windscreen at the lights ahead. In the distance, an articulated truck lumbered towards the intersection. Morrisey's Volkswagen was nowhere in sight. Margaret did not know why she was bothering to go after him.

'What am I doing?' she spoke aloud in the little car. 'Nobody's ever bothered to chase after me, for Christ's sake.'

Margaret wondered how others saw her, trying to pretend that she did not know. She knew that to them she was bitter and alone, an unmarried woman who only ever talked about work. They knew she was not one of the Beautiful People. They'd never even bothered to find out what she was really like. Honesty and kindness were qualities which, in this day and age, took a back seat to flash and show. An unlined face and a healthy tan — that's what gets you talked about ...

The car behind her honked its horn. In front, the traffic lights were still red. The truck was bearing down on the intersection, its huge tyres spraying the rain away. What was it Sam had said? The busier life gets, the emptier it is.

The newspaper clippings.

Dennis Haun.

It was never the ones you expected.

Not Sam at all. He had far too many ways of relieving tension. Anger. Drink. Self-pity. Even throwing up.

As if in a dream, she saw everything clearly. The quiet ones, the people nobody ever noticed. How could it ever have been anyone else?

She could hear Sam telling the reporters that he couldn't understand why his colleague would do such a thing. She had everything to live for.
Bullshit.

Behind her, the car impatiently blared its horn.

In front, the truck roared towards the intersection.

As she threw her foot onto the accelerator of the car, the fragile string of peel between her fingers — snapped.

Epilogue

Norris sat beneath the harsh tin-shaded lights on a scarred wooden bench. His hands were crossed nervously in his lap. He was covered in mud. No matter how hard he tried to flatten it, his hair remained standing on end. He had lost his travel bag in Gloria's sinking Subaru just before a police launch had picked them up. Norris took a look around. On the opposite wall someone had scrawled BURN THE WORLD in black crayon.

Gloria had been taken downstairs to the cells after biting a cop on the leg. The last thing she had shouted to Norris as she was dragged away was 'Have a good vacation.' He stared at the wall clock. It was twenty to six in the morning. Light was beginning to soften the sky beyond the windows of the precinct house.

The desk sergeant looked over at Norris, sniffed at the stagnant air arising from him and continued writing.

'Hello again.'

Norris looked up to see DeeDee, the Madonna/hooker/thief who had stolen his wallet, being led down to the cells. She smiled sheepishly at him. She was handcuffed.

'Looks like you'll be getting your wallet back.' She looked him up and down. 'What the hell happened to you?'

'I fell in the river,' said Norris with a shrug. 'I wish you hadn't taken my wallet.'

'Well, I'll tell ya,' said DeeDee, pulling her arresting officer to a standstill, 'stick around a coupla hours and I'll try my best to make it up to you.'

Norris cocked his head and gave her a suspicious smile. 'I haven't got anything left that's worth pinching.'

'I wouldn't say that. I told you I was a sucker for an English accent. Wait for me, huh?' She winked as she was led through the double doors to the floor below. 'Bail me out and we'll go for breakfast. My treat.'

'You can't afford it, DeeDee,' said the officer who was propelling her forward. Norris walked to the doors and watched as she was taken downstairs.

'Yes, I can,' she told him. 'I still have this guy's Amex.'

Norris smiled and leaned on the iron stair rail, watching until DeeDee had disappeared from view. Then he turned and ambled back into the waiting area as the sun began to warm the room with its light.

Read on to taste the
horror of

Christopher Fowler's electrifying
new masterpiece of one man's
descent into the abyss.

Prologue

The rain has finally ceased.

The storm has abated. Electricity still charges the acrid
air. Uprooted plants and palm leaves wash lightly at the
shore. The settling sky, which moments ago had possessed
the sealed lustre of chalced onyx, has added streaks of
burgundy at its horizon.

From a glass-smooth sea of bitter crimson she rises, barely
causing the warm water to stir about her. As she walks, the
ocean bares her shoulders, then her arms. It is as if heaven
has reached down and coupled with the brine itself; as
though the furious spume of the waves has erupted into
laden clouds to produce a golden union of sea and sky.
The woman appears as a miraculous mirage, a phantasm,
high and clear-complexioned, the planes of her face
reflecting the pearl light of the tide. She is youthful, tall
and loosely limbed, yet already in possession of a formal
grace.

She turns her face to the penumbral globe which slowly
sets behind her, her skin strangely pale in this savage
climate. Her glossed black hair is twisted along her neck
like the mane of a thoroughbred racehorse. Her slim dark
eyes are as unfathomable as the ocean from which she
rises.

As her feet find purchase on the seabed she ascends, the water returning in rivulets along her thighs and calves. Her naked body reflects the dying sun and the wine-dark colour of the sea, the colour of blood. The sanguine droplets glisten like rubies at her breast. Across her pale throat is tied a single rope of pure white pearls.

She pauses for a moment, filled with wonder. Then she closes her eyes and draws a breath. The air is spiced with lemon and brine, nutmeg and cinnamon. Her lips part in a moment of bitter exhilaration. Yet within the air she detects a loamy stench of corruption, as if the storm winds have exposed rotten roots within the freshly sundered vegetation. Soon will come remembrance, the unbearable pain brought on by loss, and the knowledge of something worse.

But for now, all is calm. The danger has passed. In the dying light she fills her lungs and slowly strides towards the waiting shore.

SUMMER

CHAPTER
1
John Chapel

✝

A sea of heat swelled against the buildings in Shaftesbury Avenue. Lurid, unnatural light flooded across the sticky pavements, lengthening the first cool shadows across ochre brickwork. It was far hotter inside the club, but nobody minded. A pair of drunken insurance executives were attempting to remember the words to 'My Way'. They leaned on each other for support, slurring and hissing into the microphone as they watched the playback phrases of the song overtake them on the video screen. Their colleagues were wedged into a semi-circle of cane chairs near the bar, their jackets removed, their shirt collars loosened. They whistled and applauded each half-remembered lyric, stamping their feet as the end of a verse was reached. The waitress who removed the mounting Sapporo cans from the table between them had her thigh stroked for the second time by a balding young man with sad eyes and sloping shoulders. As she returned to the till she made a mental note to add a fictitious round of drinks to his bill.

The song had long reached its conclusion by the time the insurance men had pulled each other back into the audience. The sweating compère, a man dressed in a pale blue evening suit more suited to a Florida wedding than a Karaoke club, unclipped the microphone from its stand. He thanked the performers and welcomed a newcomer to the stage. Her name was Linda, she was a personnel officer for — he consulted his notes — Webber-Goldtrott Merchandising — a cheer went up from a table near the bar, and she was going to sing 'We've Only Just Begun'.

The basement room was stratified into distinct groups: hard-drinking executives straight from their offices, a shrieking hen party, several rowdy birthday celebrations. Briefcases formed a leather mountain at the coatcheck. At the table near the bar, a half-stripped girl in a nurse's uniform stood beside the balding young man from the Webber-Goldtrott party. As she encouraged him to remove her blouse, a chorus of clapping began to grow faster.

'She's already paid for,' the young executive shouted in his colleague's ear. 'I prebooked her on Visa. Can I claim the cost, or should we split it between us?' He passed his group director a crumpled slip of paper.

'I hope you're joking, Caverett,' bellowed the director, glancing down at the slip, a bill for over ninety pounds. 'I'm not passing your expenses unless you give me an account to lose it on.' Lee Caverett looked crestfallen. His entire career was predicated on his ability to falsify expenses. He returned his attention to the gyrating stripper while Linda from Personnel sidestepped harmonies at the microphone.

'She's very attractive,' he pointed out. 'Makes you wonder why she has to take her clothes off for a living.'

The director was a pragmatic man. 'Because blokes like you are prepared to book her,' he replied. The stripper was now standing astride Caverett's left leg, swinging her pelvis along his thigh. She unclamped the beer from his hand and poured a little of it inside his shirt, reaching in to massage his chest. The audience's attention had now shifted from the singer to the scene unfolding at the rear of the room. The director pushed back his chair to provide more space for the off-stage entertainment. As Caverett buried his face between the stripper's breasts, the hen party released a shriek of delight. Unnoticed at the bar, two waiters were attempting to wedge a plastic bucket beneath a leaking waste-pipe.

'Where the hell is John?' asked Caverett, unable to tear his eyes from the stripper's arching back. 'Everyone else is here. I can't believe he hasn't turned up for his own leaving party.'

'You know what John's like,' said the director. 'Did you honestly expect him to show? He's not exactly gregarious by nature.'

'I don't trust people who can't relax. I've never even seen him without a tie.' Caverett drained his beer can. 'He's certainly picked the wrong job to transfer to.'

'Perhaps,' said the director. 'His honesty is going to prove a liability. People like John are pleasantly predictable. You always know where they are. At the office, at home, or travelling between the two.' He held his palm out flat. 'Straight arrows.'

'Sanctimonious bastard,' said Caverett, tearing the lid from another can. 'Good riddance. He never liked me much, anyway.'

'I don't suppose he did. You were probably too devious for him.' The director tipped his watchface to the light. 'I bet you, at this very moment John Chapel will be on Waterloo Bridge. About halfway across.'

The temperate evening currents twisted along the glowing surface of the river to rise about the cantilevered concrete girders of the bridge. John Chapel stood in the centre of the stone balustrade looking back towards the Houses of Parliament, his arms outstretched at right angles to his torso. The warm breeze embraced his cruciform body. As he shifted his feet further apart on the rough stone, he felt completely alone. A woman passing on the opposite pavement paused to watch him.

Looking up, he saw a thin parabola of cloud dipping over Westminster, one end sheened in fading sunlight, the other lost in a haze of smog. A train pulled out of Charing Cross Station, thumping between the blackened steel struts of Hungerford Bridge. Shards of shadow split the faceless buildings of the South Bank. A group of concert-goers had gathered outside the Festival Hall in a disorderly queue. He could almost hear their conversation drifting across the river.

The moment he had stepped up onto the balustrade, he had felt the sweat fade from his shoulderblades, leaving his body cool and dry. Now, perched in the middle of the bridge, he lifted his head and allowed the passing air to brush his neck, to ruffle his hair. Free from the constricting architecture of the West End, the city opened out to touch the world at its riverbanks, and the sky reached down to examine its passing sepia reflection. Watching the distant activities of other people, he felt the cramping thoughts of daily routine fall from his mind like brittle flakes of paint, returning strength to his sagging spirit.

During the recent heatwave he had stopped here every night, preparing himself for the train journey ahead. He had never felt the urge to climb the wall until this after-noon. The drop to the water was a considerable one. Reluctantly, he lowered himself back onto the pavement, dusting his knees and stooping to collect his briefcase.

Tomorrow the fine weather was supposed to break, segueing to a weekend of rain. He checked his watch, noted the remaining nine minutes before the departure of his train, and set off to the station.

Helen looked up in surprise when he entered the lounge. She was standing on the patio before an unlit barbeque stove, repeatedly jabbing at a pile of sausages. As John passed on his way to the bedroom she tapped at the glass with her fork, an irritating staccato sound. He turned and slid back the door, knowing that she was about to con-tinue their conversation from this morning.

'I thought you'd spend half an hour with them, at least. I haven't even had time to put the meat on.'

'It's too hot. They're in a basement somewhere. They booked a stripper. They're going to get very drunk. Your basic nightmare.' He dropped his briefcase. 'I don't suppose they'll even remember whether I turned up.'

'John, it's a matter of social etiquette, that's all. It's what people do when they leave a job.' She brushed a twist of ginger hair back from her eyes. 'It would have been a goodwill gesture.'

'Forget it.'

He walked back into the bedroom and began to remove his shirt, which was once more stuck to his body after three quarters of an hour spent standing in a railway carriage. As he sat on the bed to remove his shoes he caught sight of his stomach forming a fleshy concertina over his belt buckle. He tried to recall how other men appeared approaching thirty, and realised that he had no exact knowledge of his colleagues' ages. He had rarely socialised with people from the office. On the occasions that he and Helen had arranged to dine with Howard Dickson and his wife, the conversation had always revolved around company business. Discussions at home were no less consistent, rarely moving beyond the price of Josh's new school blazer, or arrangements for the weekend shopping. There were no surprises between Helen and himself. They knew where they stood with each other. He liked that.

He carefully adjusted the shower temperature before stepping into the cubicle. 'Clean towel just outside the door.' Helen had heard the taps being turned on. She was never very far away. Whenever he received a telephone call, she had the habit of replying to John's comments as if the caller was speaking to her as well. Lately he had noticed that much of their dialogue took place without the benefit of eye contact. They held mundane conversations through a variety of barriers — across rooms, between doorways, through their son. The familiarity of home life, reassuring and comfortable. He soaped his chest, leaning back against the wall of the shower to let the water run through the curly black hair covering his pectorals. Somewhere outside he could hear birdsong calling in the dusk.

In the steamheat of the cubicle, with the water beating against his face and throat, the familiar unresolved questions about their life together began to surface in his mind.

'Save me some water, won't you.' Helen was peering over the top of the shower door, watching him.

'Christ, Helen.' He sighed and closed off the taps, irrationally annoyed with her for breaking his train of thought.

The entire neighbourhood seemed to be barbequeing tonight. The air in the garden was acrid with smoke. They ate on the patio, as they had every night for a week, enjoying the last of the fine August weather. 'I assumed that we'd be together for the entire evening,' said Helen, lowering her fork to her plate and studying her husband's face. Between them sat Josh, oblivious to everything except the mound of food before him.

'We will be,' he agreed, knowing she would be upset if he worked. 'It's just that I have some studying to do before Monday.'

'There's the whole weekend ahead, John. I have a church meeting on Sunday afternoon. The house will be quiet then.'

'I won't be here either, Dad.' Josh distastefully scraped the herb seasoning from his sausage. 'I'm going over to Cesar's.'

'There you are, you'll have all the peace and quiet you need.'

'It's not as simple as that.' Sometimes he found it hard to explain his thought processes to her. 'I can't leave it to the last minute. There are dozens of clients' case-histories to read. This is a whole new field for me.'

The tip of Helen's tongue protruded between her teeth, a habit she had developed to indicate annoyance. 'John, they worked you right up to your departure date. I've hardly seen you at all in the last month. Now you want to get straight into the new job without a break?'

'It's not that.'

'Your son has started to forget what you look like. Haven't you, Joshua?'

The boy studied him thoughtfully. 'I don't have a father. I'm a half-orphan.'

'You see what I mean?'

'I know, and I'm sorry.'

'Don't be sorry, just be aware of it.' She leaned forward across her plate, searching his eyes. Her unruly red hair was still wet from her shower. 'It's no big deal. We missed you, but now you're back. We're still together, aren't we?'

'Yes,' said John, 'we're still together.'

He was searching his briefcase when Helen entered the study.

'It's just started raining. The weather wasn't supposed to break until tomorrow. What are you looking for?'

He pushed the case aside and began to search his desk. He couldn't remember picking up the company report Howard Dickson had lent him to study. The others had been fooling around, trying to get him to have a drink while he was clearing his desk.

'If you tell me what you're looking for, perhaps I can help you.'

He glanced up at Helen. She was standing before him in a pale cream dress, her freckled forearms folded across her breasts. He smiled. 'You're not going to like it.'

'Tell me quickly.'

'I have to go back to Webber-Goldtrott tonight.'

'Oh, John …'

'Howard gave me a report on the agency, its history, finances, that sort of thing. I'm supposed to study it and make notes. I know exactly where it is.' He could see the damned thing on the window ledge in his office, just where he had left it.

'Can't you get it tomorrow?'

'I've surrendered my keys. Tonight's my last chance until Monday, and then it'll be too late.'

'John, this is *exactly* what I'm talking about.'

He slammed the case shut and turned to face her. Beyond the open window rain began to patter heavily into the garden. 'What do you want me to do?'

'I don't know. There's a part of you that's never here with me.'

'It's eight o'clock. I'll be an hour and a half at the most.'

The look on Helen's face was indecipherable. She appeared hurt, scared of being excluded. He reached forward and kissed her lightly on the lips before she pulled away.

'Sometimes, when you leave ...'

'What now?'

'I think you're not going to come back. That you're just going to disappear.'

'Don't be silly. Why would I do that?'

'I don't know. Because of what happened with us. Because you feel ... buried.'

'You're wrong, Helen. After eleven years, I don't feel buried. Or anything else.' He edged her towards the door. 'I have to go.'

'Then you'd better take this.' She held the umbrella before her, a peace offering.

'Thanks. I really won't be long.' He paused in the doorway. 'Stop worrying so much.'

The sky had lowered now, the dark full-bellied clouds scratching the tops of the buildings in the Strand, heavy enough to deliver a full night of rain. He found the report lying on the sill in his overheated office, exactly where he had set it down. The building was virtually deserted. The elderly doorman called him back as he was leaving. 'Are you not going to the party, Mr Chapel?'

'No, Frank. Thank everyone for me, will you?'

'I will. And good luck in your new job. Films, isn't it? I haven't seen a film since my Edith was alive. *The Prisoner Of Zenda*, I think it was. Sounds very glamorous, anyway.'

'I don't suppose it will be.' He hovered on the step. 'It's a PR company. I'll be handling movie publicity.'

'I s'pose you'll be wining an' dining all them film stars,' called the old man. 'We'll be reading about you an' Ava Gardner in the *News Of The World*.'

'I don't think so somehow, seeing as she's dead,' muttered John to himself. Still, he wondered what his new position would involve. The salary was excellent, but Howard had been typically vague about his duties, and his hours. Whatever the job entailed, he had a disturbing suspicion that it would affect his family adversely.

He had no idea how much.

CHAPTER
2
Waterloo Station

Setting off in the direction of the station, he once more found himself heading for Waterloo on foot. There were no taxis to be seen in any direction. The bridge now presented itself as an inhospitable concrete arc, rainswept and dismal.

The station itself covered an entire city block with its crescent-shaped concourse and twenty-one platforms. The main entrance was a memorial constructed to the memory of those members of staff who had died in the First World War. Above its doors a great gold clock was set into the stone, wreathed in red ironwork. This was topped by a statue commemorating the glorious dead, surrounded by shields of the war's great battles. It had always struck him as an absurdly grand entrance for a mere railway station, more suited in an operatic setting as a portal for the dead.

Later he tried to remember the sequence of events, but never seemed able to account for every moment. The approach was deserted as he crossed the road before the worn steps which fanned up to the concourse. To the left, the angled glass roof of the curving sliproad protected a handful of passengers searching for taxis. Opposite, a battery of mounted floodlights bathed the ornate entrance in sharp white light. He remembered waiting to cross the road as a taxi approached, looking up at the battleshields and reading the names through phosphorescent needles of rain — Mesopotamia, Dardanelles, Egypt. He remembered seeing the deserted entrance lined with the roll-calls of deceased employees, the distant blur of travellers on the concourse beyond. He remembered hearing the slams of taxi doors and the crunch of gears as drivers pulled away into the sliproad. It was then that he saw her, darting through the rain, one red high-heeled shoe touching the ground, then the other, and he wondered how it was that she did not slip over. The dead white light seemed to trap time itself as she ran, freezing her from one second to the next in a series of surreal tableaux, a knee raised, then falling, the other leg outstretched.

Then she turned. Her hair swung from her neck in a glossy black scythe. Her slim dark eyes narrowed beneath an ebony fringe. Around her long pale neck was a single strand of white pearls. The rain sheened her figure in misty light.

John stood transfixed as she reached the steps. He had a fleeting impression of the look on her face, earnest and determined, late for her train. She wore a low strapless dress of sparkling red sequins that reached halfway to her knees. A tiny crimson evening bag glittered at her waist. Her polka-dot shoes sported improbably high heels. And yet the sophistication of her attire ill fitted the feral, flowing movements of her body. She raised a hand to her lips, as if she had forgotten something, lingering for a moment at the top of the steps — and then she was gone. John stepped from the kerb, his eyes still focused on the doorway ahead.

This sprite of a woman, the lightness of her body, the plucking of her balletic limbs touched something deep within him. From her entrance into the blazing curtain of rain which hung between himself and the station to her disappearance within the darkened vestibule of the terminal, the passing moments — and they could only have been moments — seemed to have decelerated to a crawl. It was as if he had witnessed a play, performed for his benefit on a grand-scale set with a single performer. And yet there was a sense of time lost, for John found himself on the white marble concourse with no recollection of crossing the road or mounting the stairway.

The girl, of course, had vanished to her platform — but which one? He glanced up at the vast destination board. WINDSOR and ETON rattled off, giving way to ASCOT, TEDDINGTON and his own stop, RICHMOND. Further around by the snack bars and newsstands, backpackers awaited trains which would bear them to Poole and Portsmouth.

Perhaps she had entered his train. As he walked along the platform he told himself he was not staring into the carriages, searching for sight of the sequinned dress. Back at the barrier the guard blew his whistle. He boarded the train and pressed his wet head back into the seat, sweating in the sultry compartment as each swing of the carriage bore him further away from the city.

What was it about her that had seized him so fiercely? He was too young to experience those menopausal pangs of envy men suffered when they passed attractive girls. Mere lust, then? Or was it the odd incongruity of allure and energy that she embodied? Whatever the answer, he would never know. She had not seen him. He would never see her again. And yet the strangeness of the scene remained in his mind, replaying through facets of his memory like a half-forgotten piece of film.

That night he dreamed of the running girl, the glittering rain, the station steps stretching steep and endless into the night. Once more he saw her fly towards the train, once more he heard her heels tick-tock across wet stone with the clarity of a metronome. The sequinned dress spun out across her pale thighs again as she turned and raised her fingers slowly to her lips, a sensual Cinderella pausing on the palace steps. The slow-motion scene was just as he had experienced it, yet something had skewed now, contorting the moment from normality into an unhealthy fetishistic image.

When the vision at last released him he awoke unrefreshed, tangled in damp sheets, to find that Helen had already risen, showered and dressed.

He sat at the study desk in his dressing-gown and briefly recorded the dream in his notebook, as though the moment would somehow prove significant. That he had taken the diary from a locked drawer made him aware that he was hiding part of himself from Helen's eyes. When she breezily entered the room a few minutes later, he started as if caught with a guilty secret. She had dressed in a smart black suit which accentuated her copper hair. On Saturdays, she worked a half day at the department store where she was a book-keeper.

'What are you doing?' She peered over his shoulder, fitting an earring.

'Nothing.' He slipped the book into a drawer and turned the key, rising. 'Why didn't you wake me?'

'You were tossing and turning all night. You looked as if you needed the extra rest.'

'You look nice.'

'Senior management are coming in. We've been asked to make a special effort. If you're not doing anything this morning, could you get some shopping?'

John stuck his hands in his pockets and stared out of the window. 'Okay. I'll take Josh with me.'

'Surely you jest.' Helen swung her bag on to her shoulder. 'He left the house hours ago. Don't you remember what you were like at his age?'

Without thinking, he said, 'I've blocked everything that happened before I was nineteen.' He had meant it as a joke, but he saw the hurt in her eyes.

OUT NOW IN
HARDBACK AND
LARGE FORMAT PAPERBACK
FROM LITTLE, BROWN AND COMPANY

Warner Books now offers an exciting range of quality titles by both established and new authors. All of the books in this series are available from:
Little, Brown and Company,
Cash Sales Department,
P.O. Box 11,
Falmouth,
Cornwall TR10 9EN.

Alternatively you may fax your order to the above address. Fax No. 0326 376423.

Payments can be made as follows: cheque, postal order (payable to Little, Brown and Company) or by credit cards, Visa/Access. Do not send cash or currency. UK customers and B.F.P.O.: please send a cheque or postal order (no currency) and allow £1.00 for postage and packing for the first book, plus 50p for the second book, plus 30p for each additional book up to a maximum charge of £3.00 (7 books plus).

Overseas customers including Ireland, please allow £2.00 for postage and packing for the first book, plus £1.00 for the second book, plus 50p for each additional book.

NAME (Block Letters) ....

ADDRESS ....

....

☐ I enclose my remittance for _____

☐ I wish to pay by Access/Visa Card

Number ☐☐☐☐☐☐☐☐-☐☐☐☐☐☐☐☐

Card Expiry Date ☐☐☐☐